GOOD GIRLS DON'T

GOOD GIRLS DON'T

CLAIRE HENNESSY

POOLBEG
FOR CHILDREN

Published 2004
by Poolbeg Press Ltd
123 Grange Hill, Baldoyle
Dublin 13, Ireland
E-mail: poolbeg@poolbeg.com

© CLAIRE HENNESSY 2004

The moral right of the author has been asserted.

Typesetting, layout, design © Poolbeg Press Ltd.

3 5 7 9 10 8 6 4 2

A catalogue record for this book is available from
the British Library.

ISBN 1-84223-175-8

Typeset by Magpie Designs in Palatino 12pt/15.8pt
Cover illustration & design by Christine Ellison
christine@paperboatdesign.com
Printed by Cox & Wyman Ltd, Reading, Berkshire

www.poolbeg.com

ABOUT THE AUTHOR

Born in 1986, Claire Hennessy spent the
majority of her childhood and adolescence with
her nose in a book or else typing up her own stories
on a computer. What little there has been of her
adulthood so far is shaping up to be pretty
similar. *Good Girls Don't* is her fifth book.

Claire lives in Dublin and can be visited
online at www.clairehennessy.com

CHAPTER ONE

I start off the summer term with a hangover, blue hair and a "reputation". The hangover is because I was out last night with Barry, and because at the age of seventeen I still haven't made the connection between excessive drinking and hangovers, apparently. I'm keeping the aspirin companies in business, though, so maybe it's a good thing. The blue hair was because I dyed it over the Easter holidays, as you do. It might have been a rebellious thing, or it might have been to match an outfit, I can't remember which. At any rate, my natural hair colour is a terribly boring, ordinary shade of brown, so it gets dyed a lot, although usually to blonde or black or something along those lines. The reputation is because of a party I held over the holiday, during which my friend (Friend? Acquaintance? Object of my affection?) Abigail kissed me, gasp shock horror, and I really wish people would get *over* it.

It's not worthy of scandal, really, especially considering that Abi has absolutely no romantic feelings towards me and was terribly drunk at the time – but because this is an all-girls school where very little else happens, it's big news. It's all *oh my gosh, do you think she's a lesbian? I've always thought she seemed the type* and awkward glances in my direction. Awkward, as if I might be attracted to *them* (heaven forbid!), despite the fact that most of them are terribly uninteresting people and unattractive on top of it. It's stupid, and slightly bizarre, too, having a mere kiss create such drama when everything that happened with Lucy went completely unnoticed. I find myself wondering what would have happened if Natasha was in my school, and the scandal there would have been while we were going out, if they're making such a fuss over *this*.

I really don't want to discuss the Abi situation with anyone, because I *like* her and she doesn't like me, not in that way, and there's something faintly pathetic about unrequited love, or lust, or whatever you want to call it. It's romantic and tragic in the movies, of course, but very few people feel sorry for the person in real life with feelings that aren't reciprocated. You just want to shake them and tell them to stop moping and to move on. Hell, *I* want to shake me and tell me to move on, and it's only been a couple of weeks.

The principal sees me in the corridor and demands to know what I'm doing with blue hair.

"It's inappropriate," she says.

"It matches the school uniform," I point out.

She gives me detention for being cheeky and tells me

2

to dye it to a more suitable colour.

Because apparently you can't learn as well as everyone else when you have oddly coloured hair. Or something. You'd think they'd spend their time doing something more productive than giving out to students about their hair or excess jewellery or something equally trivial. Oh, well, I'm too amused by it all to be angry. I'll re-dye it tonight.

We're doing RSE in our first class and discussing sexual harassment. Mary kisses John, John feels uncomfortable, John tells Mary to stop, Mary doesn't listen to him. Is this sexual harassment, girls? We all nod and agree, even though if it really happened we'd be thinking, *Nah, it's no big deal.*

Peter wants Anne to have sex with him. Anne says no. Peter says that she's been leading him on. Anne says she didn't mean to. Peter insists that she *must* want to sleep with him if she was behaving like that. Is this sexual harassment, girls?

We parrot that yes, yes it is, that no one should feel pressurised into having sex unless they want to. Never mind the fact that Anne's going to be called a tease, that she's going to feel guilty for leading Peter on, that she's going to feel as if all of this is her fault. Because that's real life, and these are stupid sheets of paper that we're reading without caring or thinking about, just delivering the expected response. Besides, it's a quarter past nine on the first morning back after Easter, and we're all half-asleep.

At break-time, Roisín comes over to talk to me. There's usually a small group of us, but it seems I'm being ostracised for today. Oh dear. If I cared, this might hurt my feelings. Nevertheless, I'm touched when Sarah and Fiona come in to talk to us. They're in a different class, and even though we're friends with them, we tend to be able to survive break without seeing them. Abi joins us a moment later, and I notice some of the girls in the class eyeing her with curiosity, wondering if that's *her*.

Honestly, people really need to get lives for themselves. My escapades are not that interesting or unusual.

At lunch we go to the shop and when we come back to school my phone rings. It's Declan. He sounds somewhat suicidal. He has pills in front of him and is wondering what the point of anything is. Despite the fact that I've heard this a hundred times from Declan before, I try to soothe him, and tell him I'm going to come to see him.

I slip out before lunch ends and tell Roisín to tell the teachers I've gone home sick. I get the bus and wait impatiently for it to drop me off on his road, then run down to his house. He takes his time answering the doorbell, while I'm standing there wondering frantically if it's too late, and then he lets me in, and I hug him.

Honestly, I spend half my time wanting to comfort him, and the other half wanting to kill him. Because right now he looks so pale and vulnerable, and yet he does stuff like this so often that it tires me out and makes me want to slap him.

We sit down on his couch and he tells me he only took a few and then stopped. I stroke his hair and hold him and listen to him while he talks about how everything just seems so futile and hopeless, and before I know it, in a rather misguided attempt to make him feel better, I'm kissing him.

It progresses to the stage where we go up to his room. He has a light touch, almost feminine. I'm thinking of Abi the whole time, until it gets to the stage where there's no more pretending, but by then of course it's too late to go back, and anyway, I don't want to.

And that's my Monday.

CHAPTER TWO

I don't tell Roisín about Declan because it'll shock her and she'll look horrified. Only for a moment, and then she'll try to cover it up. I'll say, "I know, I'm a slut" and she'll reassure me and tell me that no, no, of course not, I just got carried away, but secretly she'll be thinking, oh, Emily, how could you be so *stupid?*

Roisín is the sort of person who deliberates at length over whether or not to even kiss someone, so I always feel somewhat ashamed telling her about the sort of things I get up to. She is a believer in thinking things through, and I am a believer in following your instincts. It makes life much more interesting.

Don't get me wrong, I love her and all, but it's hard sometimes, being friends with someone who has morals. Well, I have morals. I guess. I mean, what happened with Declan was okay, because we both know it didn't really mean anything, it was just fun. It'd be different if I knew he liked me, but he doesn't. But Roisín would look at that situation and think that it was awful because we don't really care about one another, and that I was lowering myself by being with him.

It's just the way she thinks, I suppose. She's been brought up to think that way, and she's never questioned it. It's firmly ingrained in her mind that good girls behave themselves properly. It's the way most people see the world, I guess, or at least people in this school. We're supposed to be demure and good and pure and well behaved and chaste. People try to be cool and blasé about sex, but deep down most people take it very seriously, want it to be something meaningful.

It's not. Sex is sex and love is love, and they're entirely different things. The latter is what I take seriously. Love matters much more.

I think about Declan, who I most definitely do not love, and then I think about Abigail, and Hugh, and Lucy. I don't even know if that's love. They say you *know* when you're in love, that you can instinctively feel it, and I've never been sure, really, of whether it's love or just an infatuation.

I'm thinking about this during French class. French, the language of love – supposedly. Lucy's practically fluent in the language, the words tripping off her tongue like a native. It makes sense, considering it's her. She's always been good with words of love.

Meanwhile, I'm practically failing French. There has to be something symbolic in that. I don't have the skill for it, and that's why Lucy's been in a stable relationship for the past two years and I've flitted about like a bee going from flower to flower, never satisfied.

The bell goes for lunch.

CHAPTER THREE

The weather is verging on almost summer-like, so we're sitting outside. The grass is soft and the sky looks like it is too, if only you could touch it. There are loads of us sitting outside, groups spilling into other groups. I'm lying on the grass looking up at the clouds with Abi and Roisín. Sarah has her phone out, frantically texting Shane, her boyfriend. I know Shane, and I can't help but wonder how long it's going to last. He's a real charmer. I've never known him to be in a serious relationship, but then again I can't really throw stones. Still, Sarah's sweet, and I hope for her sake that it works out.

They got together on the same night my boyfriend went off with another girl. She's one of Sarah's best friends, actually, Fiona. She's in our year but I don't know her that well, only through Sarah. I think, after the initial shock and anger of him deciding he wanted to end a three-month relationship because Fiona looks good in a low-cut top, I'm mostly amused about the situation, or trying to be, anyway. I don't see it lasting terribly long, either, which I suppose is terribly cynical of me. I have very little faith in teenage relationships. They never seem to last, apart from Lucy and Andrew, but they're definitely the exception.

I look over at Fiona, talking to another girl in our year. She's not particularly attractive, but cute, I suppose, if you go for that sort of thing. I'm probably supposed to hate her for stealing my man, but I can't find it in me to care. It'd be hypocritical, considering that even though we went out that night as a couple, his mind was already on her, and I was starting to notice Abi.

I don't know what it is about Abi, really. She's got a vague air of mystery to her, I suppose, along with a hint of instability. I've seen her scars. I know she hurts herself, and there's a part of me that romanticises this. I can rescue her, be the one who saves her and makes her see how beautiful she really is, inside and out.

She's gazing up at the clouds, a dreamy expression on her face. I wonder what she's thinking about. Shane, maybe. She has a crush on him, unsurprisingly enough. He has charisma, and most girls fall for him shortly after getting to know him. I'm not sure whether I like that he's going out with Sarah, so that Abi's left available (not that it makes much of a difference, of course, but I can dream), or whether I hate it because he's chosen Sarah over her, and she doesn't deserve that.

She looks gorgeous. I feel like a creepy pervert for watching her, which makes me get annoyed with myself. Guys don't hold themselves to these standards when they're looking at girls – they don't tell themselves, "Gosh, better not look, in case someone thinks it's wrong". Even if the girl has no interest in them, it's still okay. Maybe it shouldn't be okay, but it is.

I won't look. I won't stare. I'll just resume cloud watching. There's one that looks vaguely like a fairy-tale castle, the sort where the prince and princess get to live happily ever after.

Chapter Four

On arriving home, I discover that Janet has eaten all the ice cream. This bothers me for a number of reasons, including the fact that I've been looking forward to ice cream all day, and the fact that Janet has moved out. I thought this meant actually leaving the house. Not being around. Not coming home whenever possible with laundry for Mum to do. Not eating my ice cream. Ah, my sister. I'm sure I looked up to her when I was younger, but now my feelings towards her are more along the lines of "Stop pretending to be so sophist-icated and mature and lecturing me about life when you still can't do your own washing".

I can't see me being that clingy when I'm twenty. Then again, she has a much better relationship than I do with Mum. Janet tells her everything about her life, her friends, her relationships. I don't do that. I mean, she hears the edited version of my life from time to time. In the edited version I am a perfect angel. I don't drink, I have never touched drugs, I am serious about my education, I don't flirt, I don't hold parties in the house when she and Dad are away, and I don't do anything inappropriate.

I can't imagine, for example, sitting down to discuss my current situation with her over a cup of tea. "So, Mum, I left school early on Monday to go talk my friend out of killing himself and ended up sleeping with him. Yes, I was careful. No, I don't love him. Funny thing, actually, I like someone else. She's in Fourth Year at my . . . yes, *she*, Mum. Well, there's no need for your jaw to have dropped *that* far . . . anyway, she was over here one night . . . well, two nights actually . . . no, you weren't here. I had a party . . . oh, not that many people . . . it's not a big deal . . . no, I'm sure that vase was broken *before* the party . . ."

Certainly not a conversation I want to have. So I keep quiet about anything personal and discuss school and what happened in *EastEnders* last night.

I don't really talk to Janet, either. She's doing History and Politics or something incredibly boring (to normal people, anyway) like that at university, which should give you a clue as to the sort of person she is. Incredibly ambitious and passionate about everything she sets her mind to. Loves starting intense political discussions around the dinner table just so that she can express her own opinions. She collects facts the way some people collect key rings. It's exhausting just being in the same room as her. ("Janet, can you pass the butter, please?" "Have you been following the political situation in India? If you ask me . . ." "Janet, can you pass the butter, please?" "Do you *mind*, Emily? As I was *saying* . . .")

I trudge up to my room, ice-cream-less. I have home-work to do but my bedroom is a den of distractions.

The TV, for a start. Janet got it as a present after her Junior Cert results (two zillion As, or something along those lines) and because it was too much of a 'distraction' during Sixth Year (and Fifth Year, actually – she's always been one of those odd people who actually listen when the teachers tell you to study right from the beginning), I inherited it. I bought a DVD player for myself after working for a few weeks last summer, which has only added to my general lack of productivity when it comes to schoolwork. I love movies, though. I like all stories, I suppose, but movies are special. They fuse words and images and music together to create something incredibly beautiful. I get all mushy and excited about them, wanting to hold them and love them. My walls are a tribute to that, too, covered with posters and postcards of various films, the ones that stay with you and change you in some way, even if it's almost imperceptible. Mixed in with those are the obligatory photographs-of-best-friends, so beside my *American Beauty* poster there's a framed photo of me and assorted friends at my seventeenth birthday party last December. I'm sitting on top of Barry, and Roisín is leaning on us. Andrew's tickling Lucy, and Hugh is rolling his eyes at them, as we all tend to do at the world's happiest couple. That was just before Hugh and I got together.

There's something special about going out with someone who's been a good friend of yours beforehand. You can look back on your shared history and fool yourself into thinking that there was something there all along, some little spark, and that's why this relationship is going to last forever. I'm sure we annoyed everyone with our "it was meant to be" rubbish. And it wasn't meant to be, as it turned out, and we're better off as just friends.

It was nice to fall into the fantasy while it lasted, though.

CHAPTER FIVE

There are eight of us in Fifth Year music. Sarah is in the class, which is really how I got to know her. I mean, she's been in a few of my classes since First Year, but we never really got talking until this year. We realised we had a couple of friends in common, like Shane and Hugh, which gave us something to talk about, and since she's been spending more time with them recently, what with them starting up a band and all that, I've been seeing her and her friends outside of school as well.

Seeing as Abi is one of these friends, I am rather grateful for this, but it also makes things between Sarah and me a little awkward. I get the feeling she sees me as "corrupting" her best friend, somehow, which is completely ridiculous. I've got to learn to stop being so paranoid. It's school that does it to me, I think. I go around thinking that sexuality is no big deal and that honestly, no one *cares* if you want to sleep with boys or girls, and then something at school reminds me that most people don't think that way. The way "lesbian" is thrown around as an insult. Or this girl in my class, Joanne, talking about how people who are bisexual don't really mean it. It's just a phase, or they're just trying to be different, or they're just hiding the fact that they're gay. Thank you for your opinion, Joanne. Can I hit you now?

Contemplating it gets me angry and stresses me out, though, so I don't. It's their problem, really. Besides, there are people who really don't care. They just aren't the more vocal ones.

The teacher is talking. We are supposed to be listening. Sarah and I are actually counting down the days to the summer holidays in our homework journals and sighing happily at the thought that it's only a matter of weeks until Fifth Year's over. I don't know what I'm going to do over the summer. Work, maybe. Sleep. Watch DVDs and go to the cinema a lot. Dream about Abi and other attractive people. Do a lot of hanging out and spend the three months not really doing anything, but loving it anyway. The most perfect thing about summer is being surrounded by your friends and not having any responsibilities hanging over you. The days are long and warm and gentle and it feels like anything's possible.

It's still summery outside. I look out the window longingly and am told promptly to pay attention. The teacher dislikes me because I don't give her the respect she deserves, apparently. I hate that attitude that teachers have. Respect isn't something that you're owed automatically just because you're a teacher. It has to be earned.

The bell goes, and I sigh when I realise that it's only the end of the first class of the day. The days are really dragging by. They always do at this time of the year, just when you want them to speed up.

Sarah and I discuss this phenomenon on the way to our Irish class, coming to the conclusion that the school has been cursed, so that summer always seems impossibly far away to us.

While we're waiting for the teacher to get there, she turns to me and says, "Emily?"

"Yeah?"

"Has Abi ever talked to you about . . . I don't know, anything that seemed kind of weird?" she asks.

I frown. "Like what?"

Sarah looks worried. "Like maybe wanting to kill herself?"

"She's not suicidal," I say. At least, I don't think she is.

"Are you sure?" she says. "I've been reading this stuff she's written, and it seems really dark. Maybe I'm

15

reading too much into it, but I'm worried. She never talks about what she's feeling."

"Well, she doesn't talk to me, either," I tell her.

"Really? I thought she might have. You've been getting kind of close lately."

I grin. "That's one way of putting it."

She laughs. "I was trying to be subtle, okay? But seriously . . . I worry about her sometimes."

I nod. I think I do too.

Chapter Six

She was crying because she'd just broken up with her boyfriend. She was rubbing her eyes and tear-stained cheeks and she still looked beautiful, and I took her in my arms and tried to comfort her, and the second I felt her body against mine I knew that I was seriously falling for her.

That was the night Hugh and I broke up. That was the night Abi stayed over at my house and I kissed her and then felt horribly guilty about it, because it made us both feel awkward. It didn't last, though. She didn't react the way some people would have, disgusted and revolted.

The second kiss was at my party. We were drunk. It happened. Or rather, she made it happen, and I got annoyed with her for doing it just for the shock value.

It reminded me of something Declan would do, but she's nothing like Declan, not really. Declan is all "Look at me! Look at me! Feel my pain!" and she's quiet and enigmatic. He demands attention, and she (usually, at least) shies away from it.

And Declan isn't that bad, really. I've stayed friends with him for the last couple of years, after all. It's just that sometimes he frustrates me. When he first started talking to me about how depressed he was, I told him to talk to someone who could help him, like a therapist. He said he didn't need to. I said that if he was depressed then he should, and then he got annoyed with me and didn't speak to me for a week. This happens again and again, every couple of months. I can't count the number of times I've soothed him out of doing something drastic, and sometimes I wonder why I bother. Am I making any difference? He's just going to go through this again and again. Maybe I should just ignore him and see what happens, if he'd really go through with it. When it comes down to it, it's not up to me to fix his life for him. It's up to him.

But of course I've never tried that out, because I'm not willing to risk it. He knows that, too. Suicide threats are the ultimate in emotional blackmail.

I think about what Sarah said. I don't think Abi wants to die. But what would I know? You can't know a person after just a couple of weeks of semi-deep conversations, even if you've been in the same school for years. Maybe you never really know a person, especially one who doesn't readily discuss what she thinks and feels.

I really do seem to want to play the role of the saviour, don't I?

CHAPTER SEVEN

Barry and I have a Wednesday night tradition. Wednesday is a day when neither of us gets too much homework, so I go over to his house or he comes over here, and we watch a movie. Sometimes some of the others come, too, but Lucy and Andrew are too busy being seriously stressed out about the Leaving Cert being dangerously soon, and Roisín has maths grinds (she is scarily studious sometimes, veering on almost Janet-like), and Hugh has been busy with the band and, of course, his darling Fiona, so lately it's just been the two of us.

It's a good thing, because I see Roisín at school anyway, and I see everyone at the weekends, and sometimes it's fun to have one-on-one talks with people. Besides, he likes the kind of movies I do, including *Velvet Goldmine*, which Lucy watched and said, "I'm confused. And there didn't really seem to be a plot." Whereas Barry understands the love I have for the glam rock era, and therefore the love for the movie (and the glitter and the naked Ewan McGregor), although thankfully he's over his stage of dressing like they did back then. It was a happy moment for all, I think, although he does look great in make-up.

"So what have you been up to, Miss Emily?" he asks me, as we settle down on my bed to watch *Road Trip*. (Ah, mindless entertainment!) It's a very teenage-drama-series moment, the two of us lying on the bed together, with the duvet pulled up over us, only without the sexual tension.

"Declan," I say.

"No, Emily, I'm Barry. *Bar-ry.*"

"Oh, stop, you know what I meant."

"What has he done this time?"

"Well, we sort of –"

Barry looks at me. "What did you do?"

"Slept together."

"You what?" He looks truly disgusted. I look at him carefully to see if he's joking, but he seems to be serious. That was the last thing I expected.

I can't say anything.

"Are you serious?" he continues.

I nod.

"Why?" he demands. "I mean, you don't even like him half the time. He's always manipulating you, and I can't believe you'd – degrade yourself like that."

"*Degrade* myself?" I exclaim. "I did not – no, you know what? This is stupid. I don't have to justify myself to you. I just thought I'd tell you, because you're my friend, and we *talk* about this sort of stuff. I don't need you looking down on me like this."

"I just don't see why you'd do something like that, that's all."

"Because I *wanted* to! Because it felt like the right thing at the time, that's why."

"And you think that's a good enough reason? You can't just go through your whole life doing whatever you feel like, you know. I mean, do you care about anyone except yourself?" I've never seen him this angry. It scares me.

"I do care," I say softly. And I *do*.

Maybe it's the softness that snaps him out of it. "Sorry," he says. "I shouldn't have – you're right, it's your choice, I was just being stupid."

"It's okay," I say, not meaning a word of it.

He hugs me, awkwardly. I return the hug, and then we stare at the TV screen. The tension is overwhelming.

"You know – I actually do have a lot of work to do tonight, so maybe I should go," he says.

"Okay. I mean, if you have something to do – you should get it done," I say.

He hugs me again and leaves. I close the front door after my best friend and watch him walk away.

Chapter Eight

I don't watch the rest of the movie. I consider calling Lucy, but I know she's busy studying, and I don't want to interrupt her. She's stressed enough as it is. She wants to do law, so the pressure is on.

Lucy is the epitome of the bad-girl-gone-good persona. When I first got to know her, when I was in Third Year and she was doing Transition Year, she didn't give a damn about school. We used to skip class and get drunk and/or stoned at her house. As a direct result of this, I failed all my mocks. Since then, of course, she's done a complete turnabout. From bad influence to shining star. My mum knows her mum, and she just loves telling me how much work Lucy is doing.

"Of course, she is, Mum. She's in Sixth Year."

"But she was working last year, too. You should really be doing some study this year, to make it easier on yourself next year. That's what Janet did."

"Janet can't even cook for herself, Mum."

The conversation usually ends at that point.

I can't believe Barry freaked out like that. He's never reacted like that to anything, ever. He's usually so laid-back, with an attitude like mine – if no one gets hurt, then what's the problem? And I can't believe he had the nerve to try to make me feel as if Declan is beneath me. We don't criticise one another when it comes to relationships. That's always been a given. Each of us has made questionable choices in the past, but it should never be an issue between friends.

I can't believe he thinks I don't care about anyone. That hurts. I mean, that really, really hurts in a way that I didn't think anything could. He knows me better than anyone, and he said that to me. Maybe it's true. I don't think about other people as much as I should. I don't really care about Declan, I just don't want to feel guilty about ignoring him. I don't care about my friends; I just want to have a good time with them. He's right. I'm completely selfish.

No, I'm *not* completely selfish. I try to be there for my friends, *especially* him, and I don't know why he's suddenly accusing me of not caring about people's feelings. I mean, he can hardly be feeling protective of Declan. They don't get along at all.

He just wanted to hurt me, and I don't know why, and that's what's getting to me.

We've been friends ever since First Year. He was the first friend Hugh made in secondary school, and he came home with him one day. I stopped by to say hi, seeing as Hugh and I have lived on the same road for our entire lives and we've been friends ever since we got past the "members of the opposite sex are scary and should be avoided like the plague" stage. So Hugh introduced me to Barry, and we hit it off right away. I think for a while he thought I fancied Barry, which was his vivid imagination more than anything else. I mean, I had a bit of a crush, but I was thirteen. I had crushes on everyone. I started spending more time at Hugh's house than I ever had before, and at some point Barry started coming over to see me instead. Hugh has always insisted that Barry and I are destined to be together, but then again, he's a teenage boy and he doesn't understand any male/female relationship that doesn't involve attraction.

I haven't told Hugh that Barry used to have a crush on him. Hugh wouldn't be too thrilled. Hugh is perfectly okay with the idea of girls having somewhat bendable sexuality, but it's a different story when you're talking about guys. He was disturbed enough by Barry in make-up.

That could be why Barry and I are such good friends, I guess. The sexuality thing. I don't mean that like we have some kind of exclusive club or anything, but – it was because of that common bond that we could open up to each other.

Third Year, the Lucy year. Barry and I were talking one weekend, one of the few weekends I wasn't completely wasted, and he said tentatively that he thought Hugh was cute.

"Well, of course, he's cute," I said. "That's pretty obvious."

"Yeah, but –"

"But you like him?"

"Yeah. Maybe."

I shrugged. "He's cute."

And he just laughed. "You're so cool, you know that?"

And I'd been playing it cool the whole time, but my heart was actually pounding and despite the laid-back attitude it all seemed more real and intense than most of the conversations we'd had. I wasn't sure whether that was a good thing or not, but there was a sense of relief about it all.

CHAPTER NINE

"Is everything okay?" Roisín asks me on Thursday morning before class starts.

I smile. "Yeah. Sort of."

"Sort of?"

"Barry and I had a fight," I tell her.

"Oh." She makes a sympathetic face. "What was it about?"

"Just something stupid," I say evasively. "We'll probably sort it out soon. It's not a big deal. It's just – I don't like fighting with him."

She tries to hide a smile.

"What?" I demand.

"Nothing. Just – you and Barry."

I roll my eyes. "Don't start this again. Please."

"But – you two! You'd be so cute together."

"I'm sure we would, if we had *any* feelings for one

another. People tend to forget to take that into account."

"I think there's a spark there."

"You think there's a spark everywhere, Roisín."

"Yes, but this is a serious spark."

"There's no spark. He's like a brother to me. He watches how much I drink and asks me if I'm getting enough sleep and if I'm getting all my homework done. You can't turn that into something romantic."

"But he cares so much about you," she sighs.

"As a friend! I care about you, but that doesn't mean I want to do unspeakably naughty things to you, now, does it?"

"You don't want to do unspeakably naughty things to me?" She pretends to be offended.

"Oh, sweetie, you know I do," I play along.

"Get a room," Wendy mutters as she passes by. Wendy is in our year. She's not terribly pleasant. I would probably hate her if it wasn't such a waste of my energy and if she wasn't such a pathetic person.

"What a great idea," I say sweetly to Roisín, who's rolling her eyes. "What a thoughtful suggestion, you know?"

"Very," she says, then lowers her voice. "Em – I don't know how you put up with this crap, I really don't."

I shrug. "It's not a big deal."

"Yeah, right," she says sceptically. "Still – I'm just amazed at the way you can deal with it."

"You're the sweetest person ever, you know that?"

"I try hard, I really do."

"Come on, let's go to English."

CHAPTER TEN

English. I like it when we watch movies, and read plays, and that sort of thing. I dislike the writing essays aspect of it. I mean, it can be impossible to express how much you like something sometimes, or explain why, when it's just a gut feeling that you can't elaborate on. Instinctive reactions are hard to discuss.

It's usually a fairly relaxing class, though, which makes a nice change. I'm really not that great with the whole work ethic thing, in that I don't think I have one. I just sort of drift by. Homework gets done, mostly, sometimes with time and care put into it, sometimes not.

Roisín is a good student. She wants to go into teaching, which will suit her perfectly. She's great at explaining things, particularly to those of us who are less academically inclined. (Me.) She's interested, you see, which I suppose makes a difference. She seems to like this business of learning pointless information, while I resent it.

Sometimes it feels like I'm the only person in the world who still dislikes school, while everyone else seems to have dealt with that and moved on and studied hard. Like Lucy, and Andrew, and Roisín, and Sarah. I suppose I've still got Barry for company in that area, although even he's starting to accept school as a necessary evil. But no, he understands. I still have him.

Unless, of course, I bring up last night and we start arguing again and then we never speak to one another and we end up old and decrepit and alone in nursing homes looking back at this time in our lives and wishing that we'd stayed friends instead of letting this come between us. And I don't want that to happen. The thought of not being friends with him physically *hurts*.

I'll talk to him. I'll ask him what exactly is going on, and then we'll talk about it, and we'll sort it out. Sounds like a plan.

Chapter Eleven

I see Lucy at lunch. "You're still coming tomorrow, right?" she asks.

"Of course," I smile. Tomorrow's her eighteenth, and in the time-honoured tradition of birthdays and the Irish nation, we're going to get very very drunk.

"We're meeting outside the bar at around half-eight," she continues, "but if you want a lift, come down to my house, okay? Andrew's going to drive a few of us into town."

"Does that mean he's not drinking?" I say, and as soon as I say it I wish I hadn't. Of course, he isn't going to be drinking. Not much, anyway.

She nods. "Yeah, but you know how he is about alcohol anyway. Everything in moderation, and all that."

"It's terrible, isn't it?" I smile.

She grins. "Oh yes. But anyway, just thought I'd offer you the lift."

"Sure, thanks. I'll come around at, what, half-seven?"

"Cool. And we will have a serious meaningful talk at some point during the night, because I don't think we've sat down to have a proper conversation in weeks and I miss talking to you."

"Well, whose fault is that?" I tease.

She sighs. "I know, I know. Did I mention I *hate* Sixth Year? And that I'm seriously considering dropping out and living on the street for the rest of my life?"

"You won't, though," I tell her firmly.

"I'm going crazy," she replies.

"It's only a few more weeks. You're going to be fine, and you're going to work hard, and you're going to get the points for law, and then you can relax for the whole summer."

She smiles at the thought. "Mmm. Relaxing. I like that idea."

"And tomorrow night, as well," I remind her. "Your night off."

"Yes. I will relax. I have to. Thanks, Em. I'll see you

28

later, or tomorrow, whenever."

"Right. Talk to you then," I say.

September of Third Year. I was leaving the locker room and accidentally crashed into a girl in the year above me.

"Oh, I'm sorry!" I said.

"No, I'm sorry," she said.

"Are you okay?"

"Yeah, I'm fine. Are you okay?"

"Yeah."

I laughed. "Well, I think we're finished that routine."

"Yeah. It's like you learn all these things to say, and you're not even listening to the person –"

"You're just reciting the next phrase," I finished, and she smiled.

That's how Lucy and I became friends. I saw her the next day and we chatted for a while, and after a few weeks we were constantly yapping away to one another. I thought she knew everything and besides, she was pretty. I was completely infatuated with her, but I never thought of it as a crush. It was just an obsession, I told myself, hero-worship, something along those lines. It had happened plenty of times before, and I honestly had never considered that these little obsessions could be romantic. And I never doubted that any of my infatuations with guys were romantic, because they were supposed to be. I never questioned the similarities between the two, never really noticed it. If you don't go looking for something, you won't always find it, I guess.

I looked forward to seeing her but at the same time it made me nervous, and I used to play out imaginary conversations with her in my head, directing a movie with a happy ending. I had this fantasy that she'd be crying and I'd hold her and soothe her. I'd be the one to make it all better.

One day we were talking and I was watching her applying lip balm, and I imagined kissing her. The thought shocked me so much that I couldn't focus on anything else for the rest of the day. I was walking around in a haze, not sure of anything any more.

I look back on that now and am amazed at how dramatic I was at fourteen.

CHAPTER TWELVE

I ring Barry on his mobile after school and ask if I can come over. He says okay.

It takes me twenty minutes to walk from my house to his. I'm nervous about seeing him, something I haven't experienced since the days of having a crush on him.

We do the awkward-hug thing, and then I say, "You call that a hug?" and he laughs, and it's like it never happened.

"I'm sorry," he says. "I really am. It's just – you're too good for Declan. He's an asshole, at least most of the time, and he doesn't deserve you . . . and your talent."

"What talent?" I laugh.

"I hear things," he grins.

"From who, exactly?"

"Well, Hugh, of course . . . and Michael . . . and Colin . . . and Natasha."

"Colin doesn't know what he's talking about," I grin.

"But the rest of them?"

"Oh, yeah."

"How many people have you actually slept with, Emily?" he asks.

"You know."

"No, I don't think it's ever actually come up," he smiles. "All the years I've known you and you've never given me an exact figure."

"Not *that* many," I say.

"How many?"

"I don't know, exactly," I admit.

"You don't *know?*" Thankfully, he seems more amused about this than disgusted, which makes a pleasant change from yesterday.

"I'm not keeping a scoreboard, you know."

"Well, approximately. How many? Less than ten?"

"Are we including girls?"

"Yeah, of course."

"Then more."

"Less than twenty?"

"Yes."

"Tramp." It's said playfully, but –

"That's not funny," I say.

"I was only joking. You know that."

"It still wasn't funny."

"I'm just jealous. Me with my lack of experience."

"You have experience."

"I don't think drunken nights count as experience."

"Oh, of course they do."

"Well, never with someone I loved and who loved me, that kind of experience."

I look at him. "If you're bringing love into it, then I'm about as clueless as you are."

CHAPTER THIRTEEN

We sit watching the TV curled up together. There's something so beautiful about being beside someone when attraction isn't a factor. Just friends, just pure platonic love, and an arm around a shoulder that's purely for comfort, nothing else. Maybe because it's so innocent. Lust can taint gestures, turn them into precursors to sex, rather than something simple.

And right now, sitting here with him – this is perfect. There's no tension, no wondering do-I-look-okay and what-does-he-want-from-me, just two friends enjoying a quiet night in front of the television. It's so peaceful. I could stay here forever.

My mobile rings and I answer. It's my mother, wondering where I am. I look at the time. It's nearly ten. I can't believe it.

"I'll be home in half an hour," I tell her.

"You're going?" Barry asks as I hang up.

"Yeah . . . did you realise it's nearly ten?"

"What? No way." He checks the clock. "I thought it was seven or something."

"Time flies when you're having fun," I grin.

"Thanks for coming over," he says sincerely.

"I had fun," I say.

"Me too."

Hug. Leave. It's dark out, but it's all through housing estates, so I'm safe, even if it's kind of creepy and spooky out here. And yet there's something wonderful about shadows. They're mysterious and interesting. They could be hiding anything – or nothing.

I feel like I could be in a movie. Young woman walks along deserted street at night. She tosses her hair, walks confidently. But there's eerie music playing and the shadows seem ominous, and the audience are just waiting for something to leap out and attack her. She arrives home safely, and is greeted by her boyfriend. The audience sighs in relief. Only it turns out that the boyfriend has been stabbed in the back, and he falls dead at her feet. She looks at him, and then steps over his body. A figure emerges from the shadows in the hallway, and the woman says: "Good work." The audience gasp. Maybe the figure's another woman, and they're lovers. I'm sick of movies where the women are always doing it for men, sick of women being the weak ones, too. If I ever do make movies, the women aren't going to be the victims.

I arrive home without incident, and retreat to my room. Homework is sitting there, waiting to be done. I make a half-hearted attempt at my maths before deciding to leave it, and retreat to bed.

Chapter Fourteen

Lying in bed, listening to David Bowie, and thinking about Barry. I can't even remember much of Third Year, but I know he was concerned about me. He kept telling me that he wished I'd go into school more often, as opposed to missing it to get wasted, and I kept telling him that he didn't understand. I felt sorry for myself that year, I guess. I was very much a "no one understands my deep meaningful pain" sort of girl, so I felt perfectly justified in doing whatever the hell I wanted to do. Anyone who tried to lecture me just didn't *understand*.

And he did accept it and say that it was my choice, but that he thought I could do better for myself. He does everything with the best of intentions, he really does, but sometimes I wish he'd stop thinking that he knows what's best for me.

It's not as if he has all the answers, after all. He can't even claim to be older and wiser. I'm seventeen and I can make my own decisions, even if other people don't agree with them. I do what feels right at the time. I trust my instincts. I don't take into account what everyone else is going to say or think about my choice. That's no way to live – spending your time worrying about what other people think of you? No, thank you.

Of course, it hasn't always been that way. When I first visualised kissing Lucy that day more than two years ago, *all* I could think about was what other people thought. I was so shocked at myself for being so abnormal and weird and one of *them*. I actually, although I cringe to think of it now, asked *why me*.

And it was so silly, because it was a crush, and it was fun and it was tingly and exciting, but at the same time I was terrified of anyone ever finding out. I'd be shunned. No one would ever speak to me. And once they knew, things could never go back to the way they were before. Things would be permanently changed.

Besides, I always had the old "well, I like boys, so I

must be straight" thing going for me. Because you're always told that gay people exist (although you get the feeling that despite the political correctness, it's a bad thing to be one of them) but the idea that there's something in between isn't usually discussed. It's ridiculous, because sexuality *should* be something fluid and not really clearly defined. No one's entirely straight; no one's entirely gay. Let's just say that we're all people and we all want love and affection and sex (although not necessarily in that order), and get on with our lives.

CHAPTER FIFTEEN

I wake up late on Friday morning and miss the bus, so I get into school late. A great way to start the day, I think. I'm glad it's almost the weekend, and that I have Lucy's party to look forward to.

Lucy's parties used to be very risqué. They were legendary events. She hasn't had one of those in a long time, but I think she prefers it that way. She was never really happy as a party girl. She just didn't know what else to do. We were so bored, so completely fed up.

There's one party I'll always remember, and it was because it was the first of her parties I ever went to, the first time I was exposed to anything not-so-innocent. I was barely fifteen, and I hadn't ever even touched alcohol before. I was this incredibly naïve child at this sophisticated party where everyone seemed so grown-up and worldly even though they were only a year older than me. They were so laid-back and cool and I wanted to fit in with them.

Besides, they were Lucy's friends.

The music was loud and some of them were dancing half-heartedly to it and rest were draped across armchairs or sprawled out on the floor. There was a joint being passed around, and I took a drag. The guy next to me started talking to me about something stupid, and I found it incredibly amusing, even though it wasn't that funny.

Lucy came over to us and slid in between us. "I hope you're being nice to Emily, Declan," she said to the boy.

"I'm always nice," he said.

She smiled at him and then slipped an arm around my waist. The intimacy of that action surprised me, and my face was hot. I didn't want anyone to know that I was uncomfortable with it, uneasy with what could be interpreted as a friendly gesture but which meant so much more to me, because it was her.

"Is this true?" she asked me with a grin. I blushed even more.

"Yeah," I muttered, staring at the ground.

"Emily? Are you okay?" she asked, tilting my chin up with her right hand.

I looked at her and she was beautiful and I was starting to feel nauseous and I just wanted to get out of there. I jumped up and left the room. There was a couple in the hallway, so I darted into the kitchen, which was thankfully deserted.

Lucy followed me in a few moments later. "What's wrong?" she asked.

"Nothing," I muttered.

She tilted my chin up again and said, "I think you're lying."

"I'm not," I said.

"Is it the weed?"

"Yeah, maybe."

She seemed satisfied with this. "Come back in. We're going to play Spin the Bottle."

I'd played once before at a party someone in my class had had, only then the rule had been that girls couldn't kiss girls, boys couldn't kiss boys. This game – this was a free-for-all.

And I liked it. Declan had to kiss some guy named Sean, then Lucy. Lucy spun. I watched it go, round and round, please land on me, please, please . . .

"Emily," she said. She walked over to where I was sitting and knelt down beside me. I was actually shaking with nervousness, thinking, "Right, I haven't kissed anyone since last summer and I'm pretty sure I forget how to do it and oh God what if I'm terrible and Lucy's disgusted and never even wants to speak to me again?"

And then she kissed me. It wasn't like the movies and it wasn't like my dreams, but it was nice and soft and I wanted it to go on forever, and I was disappointed when she pulled

*away and returned to where she'd been sitting as if nothing
had happened, as if it hadn't mattered.*

I was still at that age where you believe that a kiss
means something.

Chapter Sixteen

Everyone's happy on Fridays. The teachers are that
extra bit more easy-going, the atmosphere's that extra
bit friendlier. Stephanie, who's been awkward around
me ever since Monday, talks to me about weekend
plans. This type of conversation often occurs on a
Friday, I find. When you're talking to someone you
have a class with, but don't know well enough to consider a friend, you ask them what they're doing for the
weekend. You don't really care, it's just something to
talk about, a little like the "Going anywhere nice on
holidays?" topic of conversation and the "I can't
believe we got so much homework" line of discussion.
Completely meaningless drivel, really, but going
through the motions seems to make people feel like
they're doing the appropriate thing.

Roisín, Fiona and Sarah have a Business test after
lunch, so they're looking over the chapter, and I'm restless. I walk down to the shop with Abi and bring up
the Declan topic. I'm curious as to what her opinion

will be. She knows what I think of him, after all.

"Abi?"

"Yeah?"

"You know Declan?"

"Yeah," she nods.

"What would you say if I told you I'd got involved with him?"

"Involved romantically?" she says in surprise.

"More physical, less romance," I clarify.

"I'd be a little surprised," she says. "What happened?"

"He was upset. I wanted to make him feel better; stuff happened."

"Did he feel better?" she smiles.

"I think he did," I laugh. "I don't know. Do you think it's weird?"

She shrugs. "Maybe a little, considering that you don't like him that much."

"I do – some of the time."

"But sometimes people do things that don't really make sense," she continues, and I love her so much at that moment for getting it.

"What does he think about it?" she asks me.

"That's a good question," I say.

Chapter Seventeen

Lucy never dealt with anything she didn't want to deal with, and at school she never mentioned anything that went on at the parties we went to, or anything that happened at her house when we were supposed to be in school. She lived in two worlds. One was harsh and cold and real; the other was the fuzzy dreamlike world of alcohol and drugs. You never had to take responsibility in the second world, and nothing really mattered. You could just do whatever you felt like.

So she could flirt with everyone and fool around with them and let them believe whatever they wanted to believe, and it didn't matter.

We were hanging out at her friend Andrew's house, the whole lot of us. Declan was there and he was telling me about how he needed to do this because no one understood him. He had all this stuff going on, and no one got it, no one realised how much pain he was in.

I nodded. "Yeah, I know what you mean. Like, the people at school – they're all so normal and boring and they have their perfect lives and they've never known what it's like not to be perfect."

"They're just mindless sheep," he said.

"Yeah, exactly. I mean, you can only have real opinions if you step back from that mob mentality."

"If you're not part of the solution, you're part of the problem," he nodded wisely.

"They don't get it," I said.

"Yeah."

"My friend Barry – he's always lecturing me about this. Like, why am I wasting my time? And I'm like, it's my time to waste, it's my decision to make. He's got this perfect life, though, you know. He's always so happy."

"I don't get people like that."

"It's so fake," I said. "No one's really happy. People are just fooling themselves."

Across the room, Lucy and Andrew were all over each other. I watched them slip out the door.

"No one's really happy," I repeated.

I thought this was going to be like her other infatuations – short and swift. Most people in the group had hooked up at some point, and it usually wasn't serious, but it was fun. I'd had my fair share of experiences. While most of the girls in my class were going out to discos every weekend with the sole intention of finding guys, I felt safer with this crowd, where gender didn't seem to matter as much, where being attracted to girls made me cool instead of an outsider. Looking back now I suppose I have them to thank for that, at least – the sense that it was okay to 'experiment' if you wanted to, and I did.

There was this blonde girl, Izzy, who was thin and

pretty and sarcastic and very touchy-feely to begin with, so it wasn't much of a surprise when she slid into my lap one day and started kissing me. Then there was Jon, who I thought was cute but who turned out to be rather dumb. There had been others, people whose names elude me now. I thought Lucy's involvement with Andrew was going to be as short-lived as one of these flings.

I was, of course, very wrong.

CHAPTER EIGHTEEN

Andrew is driving me, Lucy, Philip, Jean, Natasha and Steven into town. I don't know the others terribly well, apart from Natasha, my ex, but since we're all squashed into the back of Andrew's car, we're getting the chance to become very well acquainted, whether we like it or not. I'm squeezed in between Steven and Jean, and Lucy's sitting half on top of me, half on top of Steven. Natasha's sitting up front because she has a sprained ankle and we graciously decided that she didn't need the extra pain of being shoved into the back.

Being this close to Lucy reminds me of the old days, the pre-Andrew days, and quite often the early post-Andrew days too, when she would giggle and smile and play with my hair and do silly things like that, silly things that were laden with meaning, at least to me.

She was plaiting my hair. I think it was blonde at that stage. She pulled every single strand away from my face, and I could feel her fingertips brushing the skin at the nape of my neck. She worked in silence, tucking every stray bit into the plait, until there was no more hair to plait. She held it in her hand, having nothing to tie it with, and twirled it around. I could feel her breath on my neck, and then her lips pressing into the skin, so briefly I might have imagined it.

Now I'm looking at her neck. Lightly tanned skin in a smooth perfect line. I've always had a thing for necks. I wonder if that's just me, or if it's everyone, or if it's because of Lucy. Barry thinks it's probably the result of watching too many vampire movies. We were discussing this once.

"Do I have a nice neck?" he wondered, looking around for a mirror to examine himself in.

I looked at him thoughtfully. "You do, actually. It's certainly above average, anyway."

"Just 'above average'?" He pretended to be offended.

"It's a great neck," I amended. "It's very pretty."

He started laughing. "Pretty? I think that's worse."

"How about 'delicious'? Is that word okay?" I grinned.

He nodded. "I think it's acceptable."

"Glad it meets with your approval, kind sir," I laughed.

"What about my neck?"

"Emily," he said sincerely, "if I was a vampire, yours would be the first neck I would bite."

"Aw, really?"

"Really," he promised, laughing.

CHAPTER NINETEEN

It's nearly nine by the time we get into town, on account of us leaving late, as groups of more than three are prone to do, and there are only a few people waiting outside. The others have already gone in. I don't blame them. It's freezing out. I'm shivering, but of course I'm not dressed for the weather in my black slutty-but-stylish dress, but for partying, so I can expect that. Besides, it's warm inside. I hope.

Lucy has reserved the room downstairs for her party, so we walk down the stairs, Natasha leaning on Jean. I see Hugh and Barry and they wave to me. I go over to them and exchange hugs with them both.

"You look amazing," Barry says.

"Yeah, you look great, Em," Hugh says.

I beam. "Thanks, guys. You're not looking too bad yourselves. Hugh, is your other half here or have you abandoned her for tonight?"

"She's getting a drink," he says.

"Good idea. I think I'll go get one myself," I say.

"Back in a sec."

I see Fiona and tap her on the back. "Hey," I say.

"Emily! Hey," she replies. "Did you just get here?"

"Yeah, I came in with Lucy and Andrew."

"Oh, she's here? I'd better go say happy birthday, then." She pauses. "You know, I know hardly anyone here, I feel so out of place. Everyone's sort of like, ah, you're Hugh's new girlfriend, and then they go back to whatever they were talking about."

"Some of Lucy's friends are a bit . . . well, they're not great with new people. Besides, they think you're an evil temptress for stealing Hugh away from me."

"I – I didn't. I mean, he –" She looks decidedly uncomfortable and awkward.

"Relax, I was joking," I say.

"I'm sorry," she says, and she really does seem to mean it. "Hugh told me that you were okay with it, but still – I feel really bad about it."

"What do you want, for me to forgive you?" I say. "Fiona, he's seventeen years old, he can do whatever he likes. So can you. You don't need my permission."

"It's just that I'd feel better if I knew you were okay with it," she persists.

I sigh. What she wants is not to have to take responsibility for what she's done, and for me to say that I hope they'll be very happy together, so she can be absolved from any guilt she might have. What she needs is to be told that she made her decision and she

46

should deal with it, but it's a party and besides, I'm not so arrogant as to think that I'm the one who should teach her a life lesson, so I tell her what she wants to hear.

"I'm okay with it," I smile, and she sighs in relief.

Chapter Twenty

I order a vodka and coke and go and sit with Barry, Hugh, Fiona and Roisín, who's just arrived. The party is at that stage where everyone's sitting with their own group of friends and no one's really mingling. I wave Natasha and Jean over to our table and introduce them.

They smile and say hi. Natasha already knows Barry from the days when I went out with her, and they start catching up. It's funny how people get all awkward after a couple have broken up. I mean, Barry and Natasha used to get along quite well, but once Natasha and I broke up, they never spoke to one another any more. Maybe it's out of respect for the ending of a relationship, a sign of recognising that something has changed and that staying friends with your significant other's friends is inappropriate, but it's just silly. There are enough horrible people in the world and not enough nice people – if you find one you should keep him or her in your life if you can. And Natasha is lovely. We're better off as friends than as anything else, I think, even though it was fun while it lasted.

The conversation turns towards politics. Roisín is in her element, being the knowledgeable type – she both impresses and intimidates me when she gets like this – and she and Natasha are having a very animated debate, with lots of emphatic gesturing.

"Who wants another drink?" I say, interrupting the discussion.

Everyone does, of course, and Barry comes to the bar with me to help carry the drinks.

"I knew you men-folk were good for something," I muse as we're bringing them back to our table.

"We have our uses," he says. "Oh, look who it is."

'Who it is' would be Declan, who's heading towards us.

"Hey," I say.

"Hey," he says. "Uh – Emily, can we talk?"

"Sure, I just have to leave these over here," I say, indicating my table. "Hold on."

Barry and I set the drinks down on the table and he just . . . *looks* at me.

"What?" I say.

"Nothing. Go talk to Declan."

"I will," I say.

"Go, then."

"I'm going." What on earth is *this* all about? I know they've never been the best of friends, but honestly, he's never been this hostile towards my friendship with Declan. And I thought we'd sorted everything out. Apparently not.

Declan's waiting for me. "Hey," he says again.

"Hi," I say. "How are you?" The second the words are out of my mouth I know it's a mistake. I don't want to know how he is. I don't need to listen to his whining right now. I need to go back to Barry and Roisín and the others and get drunk and dance and enjoy myself.

"I'm okay," he says. "I've been better."

I ignore the plea for attention for the moment and ask, "So, what did you want to talk about?"

"What do you think?" he says, as if I'm stupid.

"I don't know. That's why I asked you," I snap.

"Well, if you don't know, then I don't know what the point of talking to you is," he says huffily.

I roll my eyes. "Dec, get over yourself and just tell me exactly what you wanted to say to me."

"Forget it," he mutters, and walks off.

I'm ready to strangle him.

I'm also walking after him.

CHAPTER TWENTY-ONE

"Declan," I call after him. "Declan!"

He turns around. "Look, Emily, just leave me alone."

"Stop being such an idiot. You wanted to talk to me.

49

So talk."

"Is there anything to say?"

"You tell me," I snap.

"About what happened . . ." he begins.

"What about it?" I say.

"Well, we can't pretend that it doesn't exist, can we?"

"No, of course not."

"So . . ."

"So . . . *what?*" I say, getting frustrated.

"Well, what do you want out of this?"

"Out of what?"

He sighs. "Out of whatever it is we have."

"It's called friendship."

"Friends don't do *that* with their friends, Emily."

"Sometimes they do," I say. "It's not as if we're passionately in love with one another, is it? It just happened. You know that and I know that, so let's get on with our lives."

"You're trying to forget it ever happened," he accuses.

"I am not! I just don't see the point of dwelling on it, that's all." I sigh. "Declan, you can't honestly tell me you've never done anything like that with a 'friend' before, because I know you have. I remember."

"That was different," he says as if he's explaining something to a small child.

"Enlighten me, then," I say.

"We were stoned," he says. "It's different."

50

I don't think I have an answer to that. He has a point. But it still seems to me like an excuse for not having to accept that you've still made a choice of some kind. If you can blame weed, if you can blame alcohol, then you don't have to take responsibility for it yourself.

It's classic Declan, of course. Nothing is ever his fault. It's his parents' fault, for not loving him, or his ex-girlfriend's fault, for breaking his heart, or his friends' fault, for being mean to him or whatever it is they've done this week. It's always their fault he's so miserable. He has no control over his own life.

I sometimes wonder whether, if a psychiatrist were to analyse him, he'd be declared clinically depressed or not. I can't help but feel that if it was really that bad, he'd want to get better, but what do I know? I don't understand depression. I know what it's like to cry your eyes out or to hate yourself because you think you're a freak – everyone does when they're a teenager – but I've never wanted to kill myself. I've never looked at the world and seen only darkness. There's always a glimmer of hope in there somewhere.

"You don't have an answer," he says, almost gloating.

"What do *you* want out of this?" I ask.

"Isn't it obvious?" he says.

"No," I say, and I'm really getting annoyed at this stage.

"Are you saying you have absolutely no interest in

me, then?" he demands angrily.

"No, I don't," I say honestly.

"Even after what happened between us?"

"Declan, it was a single, isolated event! It wasn't a promise of anything more."

He stares at me. "I really don't understand you, you know."

I sigh. "Great. Thank you for that. Excuse me."

"Go play mind games with someone else, then," he calls after me.

While I make a point of never looking back with regret on anything I've ever done, I can't help but wonder if I was in my right mind on Monday afternoon.

CHAPTER TWENTY-TWO

"Well, how did that go?" Barry asks when I return to the table.

"Oh, wonderfully," I reply. "Want to help me murder him, actually? I think we'd be making the world a much better place."

"So much for all the 'he's really a nice person, deep down' stuff," he notes.

I sigh. "He's driving me crazy right now. He seems to think I have some sort of commitment to him because of what happened."

"Well, in fairness –"

"Oh, don't agree with him, please. That might just drive me over the edge."

He looks at me without saying anything.

"Okay, fine, what were you going to say?" I relent.

"Well, it's understandable that he thinks it meant something," Barry says. "Most people don't take sex so lightly, especially when it happens when you're sober. You can't blame anything for it but yourself."

"But why should you need to blame something? I mean – it's not like it's something bad."

"But it does imply some kind of a commitment. Or at least an attraction, and people assume that you'll want more from them."

I sigh. "People are silly."

"I know," he says, patting my shoulder.

"I should have been born a boy. People *expect* this kind of behaviour from guys."

"But if you were a guy, you wouldn't look half as good in that dress," he points out with a grin.

I laugh. "That is an excellent point."

"What are you two whispering about?" Roisín asks, looking pointedly at me. Her eyes are saying, "Private conversation, eh? I keep telling you there's a spark there!"

"About Emily's dress," he says honestly. "Doesn't she look fabulous?"

Everyone nods and smiles and agrees. I poke Barry and he plays innocent. "They're only being honest," he says.

I roll my eyes. "Right."

Lucy and Andrew come over to our table. "Guys, we're ordering you to dance," Lucy says.

"People aren't dancing," Andrew explains. "Come on. Be the trendsetters!"

"It's tempting, but sitting is much more fun," I smile sweetly.

"Besides, the music is terrible," Hugh adds, as a song by some pop band that sound like the latest protégés of Louis Walsh finishes up.

"It's getting better," Lucy promises, although she's sounding doubtful. "Although maybe this was why we had to pay the DJ in advance."

I hear another song start up, and clap my hands together. "Oh! Yes! Come on, Barry. We're dancing."

"What song –" Roisín begins in confusion, as people tend to when you're only three seconds into a song.

"'Suffragette City'," Barry says, getting up. We're the only ones on the dance floor at the start but we're still having fun. There's something special about hearing one of your favourite songs when you're out somewhere, something that's different from hearing it at home. By the end of the song there are a few others dancing, although none quite as enthusiastically as Barry and myself.

"You know what's terrible?" I muse after the song ends.

"That Bowie is now a respectable suit-wearing musician?"

"Yeah," I grin.

"What we need is a time machine. We can travel back to 1972 . . ."

"Back to the days of stardust," I say.

"The days of bad hair."

"The days of glitter."

"The days –"

"You two really scare me sometimes," Lucy grins, having sneaked up behind us.

"We're not scary," we say in unison.

"We're just in denial about the suits," I say.

She pats our heads. "There, there!"

The song that's playing now is 'Every You Every Me' by Placebo, and as we're dancing, I find myself thinking about the first time I heard it. It was at *that* party, the one where Lucy and Andrew got together. For months, that was all I associated the song with. I got over it, though. When I could listen to it without getting an ache, that's when I knew that I was finally getting over her.

CHAPTER TWENTY-THREE

"Hey, Barry?"

"Yeah?" he replied.

"Remember a couple of weeks ago when you were talking about Hugh?" I said tentatively.

"Yeah," he said, looking almost defensive.

"Do you still – think that?"

"Yeah, why?"

"I was just wondering."

"You haven't said anything, have you?"

"No. No, I haven't. And I won't. You know I won't." I paused. "You know Lucy?"

"Yeah. Well, not really, but – yeah."

"She's started going out with this guy Andrew. They're, like, madly in love or something."

"Do you like him?" he asked, picking up on the bitter note in my voice.

I shook my head.

"Do you like her?" he asked.

I nodded, and, nonchalantly, doing what I'd done a few weeks before, he said, "She's cute."

Only I didn't laugh. I just nodded again and said, "Yeah."

He didn't say anything, but he moved closer to me and let me rest my head on his shoulder, and we stayed like that for the rest of the evening.

"How many days have you missed so far this month, anyway?" he asked.

"Most of them," I shrugged. "Look, Barry, I don't want to go in there. You don't know what it's like. It's just too much right now."

"Look, I know school isn't exactly fun, but you've got your mocks next week and you haven't even been in school for a full week since before Christmas."

"They're just the mocks," I said. "Besides, no one can determine your intelligence from one stupid test."

"They're not trying to. They're just seeing whether you've paid attention for the last three years or not, and yeah, it's a pain and it's completely stupid, but you're going to have to do the exam no matter what."

"Stop lecturing me, Barry. I don't need this."

"I wasn't trying to lecture you, Em."

"Well, then, don't! I'm getting enough of this crap from the teachers. Work hard, study hard, blah blah blah. It's too much. They don't understand. They don't care about what I'm going through."

He just sighed. "Yeah. I know."

"Okay, you were right and I was wrong."

"What?" he said.

"I failed everything," I told him.

"Oh. Everything?"

"Everything," I confirmed.

57

"Well, at least they're just the mocks," he said reassuringly.

"Yeah," I said. "That's what my mum said. She was pretty annoyed, though."

"I bet."

"So, starting from next week, I'm not allowed out until after the Junior Cert," I said, "except for the Easter holidays. I can't believe she's doing this to me. It's so unfair." She was cutting me off from everything and everyone – including Barry, who was keeping me sane about the whole Lucy thing, and Lucy herself, whose company I still desperately craved despite the fact that she and Andrew were inseparable now.

"She just wants you to study, though."

"Yeah, well, maybe I don't want to."

"But if you're not allowed out – well, maybe you should do a bit of work. I mean, if you're stuck inside, you might as well try to pass the exam, you know?"

"I suppose," I said sullenly.

"Or you could just sulk," he suggested.

"Stop treating me like a kid," I told him firmly.

He grinned. "Kids are easier to talk sense into."

"I'm taking that as a personal insult, mister."

"Good, you were supposed to," he teased.

I laughed, and then tickled him until he begged for mercy.

Chapter Twenty-Four

Hugh and Fiona join us on the dance floor after some time, and I watch the two of them together. They both look happy. I wonder if I ever looked that happy when I was with him. I did at the start, I suppose. We were both so happy and giddy and euphoric.

New Year's Eve and we were all at Shane's party. Barry and I were talking and he said that I should kiss Hugh at midnight.

"Hugh? Hugh?? Hugh? You're not serious."

"Oh, come on," he said. "You like him, I know you do."

"I do not," I said coyly.

He looked at me sceptically. "Emily, that was a pathetic denial. I wasn't even momentarily fooled."

I laughed. "Okay, okay. I like him. But he'll run away screaming if I try to kiss him."

"I don't think he'll be doing that, somehow," Barry said mysteriously.

"Do you know something?"

"I might," he said, smiling.

"Tell me!" I demanded.

"No, it was told to me in confidence," he said.

"Sharing is caring," I wheedled.

"Well, let's just say that Hugh wouldn't be entirely

opposed to the idea of you and him in some kind of romantic embrace . . ."

"Did he tell you that?"

"My lips are sealed," he said.

"So that's a yes, then," I smirked.

"Yeah," he admitted. "But don't mention to Hugh that I told you. You're supposed to be seducing him of your own accord."

"He'll never know," I promised.

"Ten! Nine! Eight!"

"Hey," I said, sauntering over to Hugh. I was in a short black skirt and a shimmering blue top and I knew I looked good. I'm confident, I'm cool, I thought.

"Hey," he said back.

"Four! Three!"

I smiled.

He smiled.

"One! Happy New Year!"

Everyone was cheering, and he grabbed me and we were kissing and clinging to each other and it was like I'd been waiting for this my whole life, because it made so much sense. It was Hugh. He'd been a part of my life for so long and now – now I had him.

And I'd never felt so happy.

"What's great about it," I explained to Barry the following week, "is that we've known each other for so long that we're *completely comfortable with one another. It's just amazing. I mean, he knows so much about me, and I know so much about him, and we don't have to learn any of that stuff. We just know it already. But it's still passionate, you know? I'm still really attracted to him, even though we've been friends for so long. It's the best of both worlds, really. I think maybe that there's always been something there, and sub-consciously we've always known, but it's taken a while for our conscious minds to grasp it. Don't you think?"*

He nodded. "I'm happy for you guys."

I hugged him. "Thank you. That means so much to me. You know, I'm really glad you told me I should go for it. Otherwise I mightn't have plunged into this the way I did. Well, knowing me, I probably would have, but I wouldn't have seen it as being a long-term thing, it would have just been something casual. But this means something, you know? I seriously think this is the sort of thing that could last for a really long time."

"That's really great, Em."

I beamed.

That was at the start, of course.

CHAPTER TWENTY-FIVE

"My feet are getting sore," I tell Barry. "I'm going to go sit down for a while."

He nods. "Want me to come with you?"

"Nah, it's okay," I smile.

"It's your own fault for wearing those shoes, you know," he grins.

"I know. They're completely impractical but they're so *pretty.*"

I sit back down at our table. Natasha's there, with Jean and Steven beside her. "Hey," she smiles, "looks like you were having fun."

I nod. "Yeah, but these aren't really dancing shoes."

"Oh, it doesn't matter. They're pretty," she says.

"That's exactly what I told Barry," I laugh.

"What's the deal with you two, anyway?"

"What do you mean?"

She stares at me for a moment. "You know what I mean, Emily! You two! When did that happen?"

"What? Nothing – *happened.*"

"Oh, come on."

"No, seriously. We're friends. We've always been like that."

"No, I remember you two as friends. You've never been quite this close. You've never looked at one another that way. You're kidding me about not being with him, right?"

"I'm not," I say. "Really, we're just friends. It's Barry. He's like a brother to me."

She raises her eyebrows. "God, I hope my brother doesn't look at me that way. I'd be pretty scared."

"We have a completely platonic relationship," I tell her. "Not everything's about lust or love."

Natasha laughs. "I can't believe I'm hearing *you* say that."

"Oh, stop. I'm not that bad."

"Yes, you are," she grins.

"Only sometimes."

"I still can't believe that you and Barry aren't together. I mean, you're perfect for one another."

"That's what people seem to be saying," I sigh.

"And you don't think that if people are saying it, maybe they're right?" she says.

I shrug. "I'm not attracted to him. That's what it comes down to. He's my dearest friend in the whole world and I love him, but that's as far as it goes."

She smiles. "Okay. What about you and Hugh? What happened there? The last I heard, you two were all over each other. What's he doing with this Fiona one?"

"Hugh and I broke up," I say.

"Well, obviously. But what exactly happened?"

"He liked Fiona, so – he went off with her."

She makes a sympathetic face. "What an asshole!"

"Yeah," I say, not really meaning it. "We'd been having problems before that, though."

Problems. We had our parents getting involved in our love lives, for a start. They found out that we were going out and were delighted about the whole thing, and decided that the best way to encourage this blossoming relationship was to interrogate us about it whenever possible.

That wasn't really an issue, though. It was more about – well, sex, really. It's starting to seem that everything is, really.

Chapter Twenty-Six

"I don't want to rush things," Hugh said. "I mean, what we have, it's something really special, and I don't want to ruin that."

I nodded. "Of course. We'll take things slow." I smiled at him. I'd been smiling non-stop for the past week or so, ever since New Year's. Roisín had told me that it was truly sickening how happy I was, and had taken to making "awww" noises every time Hugh and I were near her.

It was vaguely irritating but mostly just appropriate for how we were both feeling.

"This is going to be perfect," he said.

"Perfect," I echoed.

"Barry, you're my best friend in the whole wide world, right?"

"Right," he nodded.

"Sleep with me."

"What?" he said, looking appalled.

"I'm not that hideous, am I? Come on, as a favour to me.

64

I don't think Hugh has been told about the birds and the bees yet and I'm feeling incredibly deprived. He won't mind if it's you."

"Emily, you're being ridiculous."

"Maybe if we watched some porn," I mused. "That'd do it. Do you have any videos I could borrow?"

"No! Do I look like the sort of person who has a porn collection?"

"Male, teenage – yes!"

"Emily."

"Help," I said dramatically, throwing myself into his arms.

"I only hope you know how melodramatic you're being," he told me.

"Yes, I'm sadly aware of that fact. But seriously, Barry, we've been together for two months, and – nothing! We never even get the chance to do anything. It's depressing. I'm starting to think he's not remotely attracted to me."

"Oh, don't be silly. You're gorgeous. He's crazy about you."

"Really?"

"He's just nervous."

"About –"

"Well, you know he hasn't ever – you know."

"Seriously?" I was truly taken aback by this. Hugh had always hinted at encounters, and I'd assumed he'd slept with girls before.

"Yeah. He talks big, but –"

"I can't believe he never told me that," I said.

"It's not that surprising."

"Yes, it is! He's very attractive, and –"

"No, I mean it's not surprising he hasn't told you about it."

"Do you think he feels inferior or something?"

Barry nodded. "Well, obviously. I mean, you're so laid-back and casual about everything, and you've had all this experience –"

"Not that much."

" – and although you mightn't think it, occasionally guys get insecure about that sort of thing."

I feigned amazement. "No way. Guys have feelings?"

He smiled. "It's true, I'm afraid."

"So what do you think I should do? I don't think he'd want me to tell him, 'Don't worry. I don't mind if you're a virgin'. Even though I don't."

"Do whatever feels right."

"That's what I've been trying to do. That's why I'm here propositioning you," I laughed. "Speaking of which, I'm very hurt that you turned me down."

"Only because of Hugh, I assure you."

"Oh, well, in that case."

"It's going to be great. You know how talented Shane is, and then Sarah has that amazing voice, and . . . I mean, don't you think that we have a chance of making it?"

"Oh, yeah, definitely," I said, smiling enthusiastically.

"It's always been my dream to be in a band," he continued.

I decided not to point out that he had actually wanted to be an actor at the age of eleven, and that by the age of twelve he'd decided he was going to be a doctor and save thousands of lives, and that because Science was too much work, he had decided at thirteen to be a professional skateboarder, and at fourteen he wanted to be like the guys on Jackass.

"You know," I laughed, "all the girls will be after you now that you're in a band."

"And they'll be jealous of you for having me," he replied, putting his arm around my shoulder. I leaned in to kiss him, but he didn't seem interested. He just wanted to talk.

"Is he gay? Is he gay and just not telling me? Because, honestly, I don't mind if he's using me, because he's incredibly sexy, but I do want something in return for all of this. He talks. He talks and he talks and he talks. This isn't normal, Barry. It's scaring me. I was brought up to believe that boys are an evil corrupting influence that are only after one thing, damn it!"

"Emily, remember what we said before about the melodrama?"

"He won't shut up about the bloody band! That's all I hear about! And every time I see Sarah in school she's yapping on about it as well. It's driving me up the wall. I want a boyfriend who'll try to get my clothes off, not one who tells me I'm pretty and smart. I mean, 'pretty'? 'Pretty' is for shoes and dresses and wallpaper. It's not for the object of your lust. And smart? I don't know where he's getting that from, but it's not a turn-on."

"Have you ever considered the possibility that you're a nymphomaniac?"

"Every day of my life."

"I'm not surprised."

"A girl has needs, Barry."

"Talk to him."

"I've tried. He just changes the subject."

"It can't hurt to try again."

"I suppose."

"Or, failing that, I suppose I'll volunteer myself to show him how it's done."

"That means a lot to me, Barry."

CHAPTER TWENTY-SEVEN

"I think we can add Natasha to the list of people who think we're destined to be together," I tell Barry as I return to the dance floor. "It's clearly fate. We should probably just declare our love to the world."

"You're right," he nods. "The people deserve to know the truth."

I laugh, and twirl around. "It's crazy, though, isn't it?"

"Not really. We're close. People assume it's more than what it is."

"Yeah, I suppose."

"And people are silly."

"Yes, yes they are," I say. "Especially Roisín," I add, noticing that she's giving me more pointed looks. "She thinks there's a spark between us. There's no spark."

"No, no spark."

"People are just . . ."

"Silly."

"Hey, what time is it?"

"Nearly three."

"Yeah, that'd explain the tiredness."

"Are you getting a lift with Andrew and Lucy?"

"I think so. I don't know when they're leaving, though."

"We could get a taxi."

"Yeah, we could."

"We could."

"Or."

"Or we could do something crazy."

"We could start dancing on the tables."

"That's old. People were doing that earlier."

"We could show off our Irish dancing skills."

"What skills?"

"Exactly."

"We could sing."

"Oh, that's just cruel. We couldn't inflict that on people."

"You're right. They'd never recover."

"We could start a food fight."

"There's no food left, though."

"Ah, forget it. I'm tired."

"Come on. Let's go home."

We wish Lucy a happy birthday once again and wait outside for the taxi. It's freezing, and I am in my impractical dress. Barry, being chivalrous and also sick of hearing me whine about the cold, offers me his coat.

I think about what everyone says about the two of us, and how they'd be greatly amused to see me wearing his coat. And it would be romantic – if it wasn't him.

CHAPTER TWENTY-EIGHT

I sleep gloriously late on Saturday morning. Lie-ins are the ultimate luxury, I think. Especially when you're sensible the night before and drink in moderation. Ah, being sensible. It's not something I have very much experience with but it seems to be a good thing.

Janet's at home for the weekend, naturally, and she's sitting at the kitchen table eating her lunch when I go downstairs. Lunch, because of course she's been up since eight and has already had her breakfast.

"That can't be healthy," she says as I help myself to a chocolate mousse.

"Probably not," I agree.

"Aren't you going to eat anything else?"

"Well, I would be having ice cream, but you ate all of mine."

"Oh, don't be so childish."

"Childish? Me? I'm not the one who's still pathetically clingy at the age of twenty."

"I'm not clingy, Emily, I just enjoy spending time with my family. You'll understand when you're older," she says condescendingly.

"You're three years older than me. Get over yourself," I tell her.

She just sighs and shakes her head in that I-know-better-than-you-but-I'm-going-to-be-mature-and-leave-it sort of way that she does so well.

I want to pull her hair or slap her across the face, but I wisely decide not to. She'd fight back.

She has a superiority complex because she's incredibly smart. I really don't think that's enough of a reason to act like you're better than everyone else, nor do I think the educational system is based on intelligence. It's mostly based on an ability to learn off by heart and then regurgitate the information within a short space of time.

I really dislike exams. Of course, I can't ever express

this dislike around her, because she'll start talking about how everyone has to do them, and they test how much you *know*, and blah blah blah. Whenever she starts talking about any of her passions, I have to tune her out. It's the only way to stay sane.

Which is why I go and eat my incredibly healthy breakfast in front of the TV. I'm sure she'll be in later to ask me why I waste my time staring at the idiot box, but for the moment, she's leaving me alone, and it's peaceful.

CHAPTER TWENTY-NINE

The phone is ringing. "Emily, it's for you," Janet calls from downstairs.

I pause *Amelie* and go down to the hall, accepting the phone. "Hello?"

"Hey, Em, it's Lucy."

"Hey, how's it going?"

"Great, everything's great. Did you get home okay last night?"

"Yep, the taxi came after about twenty minutes."

"You seemed to be enjoying yourself," she says. "You and Barry."

"Lucy, don't start."

She laughs. "Okay, I won't. Anyway, since I didn't

get much of a chance to talk to you last night, do you want to come over sometime today? I have pizza."

"Pizza, you say?"

"Yes."

"I'll be there," I laugh. "I'll see you in a while. I just have to get dressed."

"Oh, don't bother. Come naked," she giggles.

"Now *there's* an idea."

"See you."

"Bye."

"Do you love him?" I asked her one day when it was just the two of us.

She smiled. "Yeah. I really do."

"I'm pretty much grounded until after the Junior Cert," I told her.

She made a sad face, but I wondered if she really cared. "But that's so unfair."

"Yeah, I know. But there's not much I can do about it," I said.

"You can just not listen to your parents," she said. "What can they really do to you, anyway?"

"Lock me in my room? Stop feeding me? Kick me out of the house," I suggested.

"You could come live with me," she smiled.

"I'd get in the way," I said in a very self-pitying sort of tone.

"*Of course you wouldn't! You're one of my best friends, Emily.*"

"*Yeah.*"

"*You are.*" *She kissed me lightly on the cheek, then the lips.*

I pushed her away. "*Don't touch me, Lucy.*"

She was taken aback. "*What's wrong with you? You know I'm always like this —*"

"*Well, maybe you shouldn't be,*" *I told her angrily.* "*I mean, you go around playing mind games with everyone and flirting with them, and you think it's okay. Maybe it isn't.*"

"*Everyone knows I don't mean it, Em,*" *she said softly.* "*No one takes it seriously.*"

"*Right,*" *I muttered.*

She closed her eyes. "*Oh, no.*"

"*I have to go,*" *I told her.*

"*Emily, I — I'm sorry,*" *she said.*

"*I have to go,*" *I repeated, and walked out the door.*

She's wearing jeans and a see-through shirt with just a black bra underneath it. On someone else it might look ridiculous or inappropriate for a Saturday afternoon. On her it just looks elegant.

"Hey," she says.

"Hi," I reply.

"I have pizza, as promised, and I've tidied my room just for you."

"Your room's always tidy," I point out.

"Well, it's especially tidy today," she laughs as we go in. "See?"

"You're such a neat freak," I tease.

"I know. It lets me fool myself into thinking that my life's okay. You know, if everything in my room's in its rightful place, everything else is too."

"Is everything okay?" I ask her.

"Yeah. Kind of."

"Kind of? How are things with Andrew?"

"They're . . . I don't know. Confusing."

"Confusing in what way?" I ask.

She shrugs. "I've been going out with him for two years now. That's a long time. I mean, I hadn't even turned sixteen when I started going out with him. And we were both really different people back then."

"Yeah, I know."

"And we've been through a lot together, you know? We started off as kids, and now we're – well, not grown-ups, really, but getting there, closer than we were before. But we've both changed so much . . ." she trails off. "I'm not even sure what I'm trying to say here. I still love him, honestly. But I've been thinking about all this lately."

"It's birthdays. They do that to you," I say.

"Do you think I'm too young to be tied down?"

"Lucy, you're asking the wrong person here," I tell her. "Do you really feel 'tied down', though, or just committed?"

"I don't know," she sighs. "Emily, help! You're good at this stuff. Tell me what I'm feeling."

I laugh. "You're having a coming-of-age crisis."

She smiles. "That must be it."

We sit in silence for a moment before she asks, "So, what's going on between you and Declan?"

CHAPTER THIRTY

Third Year, a Saturday night a couple of weeks before the mocks. Declan and I were talking and out of the corner of my eye I was watching Lucy and Andrew. They were intensely engrossed in conversation, and every so often they'd stroke the other's cheek, or kiss their neck. I'd never seen two people more in love.

I wanted to go over there and tear them apart and tell them to stop acting so intimate because it was sickening, and because every time they touched one another, I wanted to cry.

"If you were going to kill yourself, how would you do it?" Declan asked me.

I shrugged. "I don't know. Pills, I suppose."

"Yeah, me too. Although there's always hanging yourself."

"Or slashing your wrists."

"Do you know the right way?"

"There's a right way?"

76

"Yeah," he said, eager to impart this information to me. "See, most people, when they're doing it, slash across."

"And that's wrong?"

"Yeah, you're supposed to go along the vein. Lengthways," he said, turning my hand over and dragging his fingernails lightly down my wrist. "Then you're supposed to make a couple of little gashes across, so that it can't be stitched up quickly."

I nodded. "I see," I said, recording the information in my mind. I had no intention of ever making use of it — I hoped — but even having this knowledge seemed to give me a power. The power to say, "Hey, I know how to kill myself properly. I've thought about this. Does that scare you? Does it?"

"Do you think about it much?" he asked me.

"Not much," I said, but not elaborating. What I meant was, not ever, but somehow I got the feeling he'd think less of me if I said that. "How about you?"

"Every day," he answered.

"Haven't you thought about getting help?"

"Help?" he said scornfully.

"Yeah, like counselling, or something."

"That's not going to help me," he said dismissively. "Besides, I don't need it. It's sort of pathetic, don't you think? Talking to a complete stranger about your problems? And it's not like they really care, anyway. They're just listening because they're being paid for it. The whole idea of therapy is stupid. It's just a way for people to make money. It's sad, that's what it is."

"Yeah" was the only thing I could think of to say. I'd never really looked at it that way before. Declan was always thinking about these things. He had all these opinions on things I'd always taken for granted without questioning them.

"It's something that's become really popular because everyone thinks they have problems and need to see a shrink," he continued. "And most of the time they don't, they just think they do. Take the girls in your school, for example. They have, like, perfect lives, but I bet they think that their lives are so awful when they can't find anything to wear or someone doesn't like them or something stupid like that."

"Yeah, they're so superficial," I agreed.

"People like you and me, Emily — we understand what's really important."

I nodded, even though I didn't really get what he meant at that stage. But I wanted to be a part of it. I liked what he was saying.

"We see the world for what it really is, and they're stuck in their little bubbles, protected from everything," he said.

"They're children," I said. "They're never going to grow up and realise what life's really about. They're just going to stay like that in their fantasy world forever."

He looked at me, impressed. "Yeah, exactly."

Ah, the joys of being a pretentious pseudo-intellectual fifteen-year-old.

CHAPTER THIRTY-ONE

"I'm going to do it tonight," he told me.

"No, Declan, don't."

He stared at me. "There's nothing you can say to make everything better, so don't even try."

"I have to try. You're my friend."

"You don't really care about me."

"Of course, I do. That's why I'm here, isn't it? That's why I'm talking to you, trying to make you realise what you're doing."

"It's just so you won't feel guilty when I go through with it."

"No, it isn't. Don't, please. Look, I'll stay here tonight. We'll watch a movie or something. We'll listen to music. We'll have fun."

"Fine," he conceded. "But I don't know why you think it'll make a difference."

I wanted to snap at him and tell him that I was trying to help him and be his friend and be there for him, and that maybe, instead of being mean, he should be grateful. But I was scared of setting him off, so I said nothing.

My phone was ringing, and I sleepily reached for it, chastising myself for not turning it off before I went to bed. But then again, what if someone – like Declan, whose caller ID was coming up on the screen – needed to talk to me? So I had left it on.

"Hey," I said.

"Hello," he said, sounding distant.

"Is everything okay?" I asked.

"I just wanted to say goodbye," he said in that same distant tone.

"Oh, Declan. No. You haven't done anything stupid, have you?"

"I have to do it, Emily," he said.

I breathed a sigh of relief that he hadn't actually done anything yet.

"No, you don't. Think of everything you've got going for you. You're smart, you're attractive, you're interesting —"

"Don't lie just to try to keep me alive."

"I'm not lying. Don't be silly. Would I lie to you?"

"You might, if you thought it would do any good."

"I just don't want you to waste so much potential," I said. "You've got your whole life ahead of you. The whole summer, even. No school for months — tell me that isn't a cheerful thought."

"It just means I've more time to be bored and think about things," he said miserably. "Do you want to do something tomorrow?"

"I can't, I have my maths exam."

"Your exam?"

"My Junior Cert, Declan?"

"Oh, right." He paused. "You should really get some sleep."

"Yeah, I hear that's a good thing to do."

"Goodnight, then."

"Night," I said, throwing the phone across the room and burying my head in my pillow in an attempt to speed up the process of falling asleep.

"Everything in life is so futile," he said. "You're born, you go to school, you work, you get married, you die. You're just going through the motions. It's such a waste."

"That's a pretty pessimistic view, Declan," I said.

"It's realistic," he said glumly. "Take you and Natasha, for example."

"What about me and Natasha?" I said warily.

"Well, you've said yourself that you know it's not going to last. If that's the case, then why bother? What's the point in wasting your time?"

"It's fun," I shrugged. "I like being around her. Even if it's not going to last forever, it's what's making me happy at the moment."

"It must be nice to be happy," he said.

I'd known him for a year. I'd seen him happy before. Often it was due to being under the influence of various substances, but other times I'd seen him smile and look content, and then hide it, as if he was afraid someone would see and realise that there was more to him than being depressed.

It was the attitude that a lot of that crowd shared,

this need to be permanently down and dour. Once I'd stepped back from it, I'd started to see them for what they really were. Apart from Lucy, Andrew and Declan I wasn't really friendly with any of them any more. I'd made a couple of new friends in school since September. It was Transition Year, which seemed to be consisting mostly of time-wasting and gloriously non-academic activities, so there was plenty of time to get to know people that I hadn't really talked to before. There was this girl Roisín who I'd always pegged as one of the serious academic types – the sort that I avoided like the plague after having Janet as an older sister – but once we'd got talking, we seemed to agree on a lot of things. She was sort of sheltered, but I thought it was endearing in a way. It certainly made a difference from the cynicism and the jadedness of Lucy's friends.

She didn't strike me as the sort of person who thought the world was such a terrible place that the only way of dealing with it would be to remove your-self from it completely.

But I couldn't just ignore Declan. I couldn't take the risk that one day he'd actually follow through on his promises.

CHAPTER THIRTY-TWO

"Well," I begin. "I want to strangle him. So the usual, really."

"He is a bit of a pain, isn't he?" Lucy sighs. "The poor guy, though, he's got so many problems."

"He creates them for himself," I say bluntly.

"That's a bit harsh."

"And I'm tired of being nice," I sigh.

She strokes my hair. "He'll grow out of it. Eventually."

"Is that a guarantee?" I ask.

"Or your money back," she laughs.

I look at her now and she really hasn't changed much since the first day I met her, two and a half years ago. She's a little bit prettier, and she's replaced her cute-sexy-schoolgirl look with a sophisticated-almost-college-student look, but she looks basically the same.

The real change was inward, although to anyone who really knows her, the change isn't as drastic as you might think. Lucy at eighteen is still a flirt, still fun to be around, still giggly. A lot more responsible than she used to be, I suppose, but that happens to everyone.

It was two years ago, during the Easter holidays, so I was allowed out. My schoolbooks had been put aside for the two weeks and I was ready to enjoy myself, only I'd realised that my world had become a lot smaller in the last couple of months. I'd alienated most of the girls in my class during my days of hanging around with Lucy and her friends, and now that I no longer had them in my life, there were very few people that I was close to.

Not that I'd ever really been close to any of them. I still had Barry and Hugh, and they were all I needed, even if I missed Lucy. We talked on the phone occasionally but this was usually when she was drunk and she ended up rambling on and never making much sense. I daydreamed about her in school when I was supposed to be listening to the teacher, and then I'd snap out of it, worried that people would somehow be able to see what I was imagining.

Three days into the Easter holidays, she rang me.

"Emily? Emily, are you there?" She sounded panicked.

"Lucy, is that you?"

"Yeah, it's me," she said. *"Emily, I'm in serious trouble. I don't know what to do."*

"What's wrong? Lucy, tell me, what happened?"

"I'm so stupid! I should have thought!"

"What did you do?" I asked her, my heart pounding.

"I think I'm pregnant," she whispered. *"Emily, I'm so scared, I don't know what to do. If my mum finds out, she'll kill me."*

"Have you done a test or anything?" I asked.

"No, not yet. I don't even know where you'd get one," she said.

"Boots would have them."

"They'll look at me," she said hysterically. "They'll look at me and they'll know, and they'll think, 'what a stupid slut' and they'll be right, I am, and I'm going to be just another statistic and I'm going to have my whole life ruined and oh, God, Emily, I'm scared."

"Breathe, okay? Just breathe."

"I'm trying!"

"I'll be over to see you in a little while, okay? Make yourself a cup of tea or something. We'll sort this out," I told her.

"Thank you," she sniffed.

CHAPTER THIRTY-THREE

"You want to watch a movie?" she suggests as we go downstairs to the family room.

"I don't know, Lucy. You know how I hate the film industry," I grin.

"How does *The Talented Mr Ripley* sound to you?"

"Jude Law? Sounds good."

"Or we could watch *Girl Interrupted*."

"That movie depresses me. Although, Angelina Jolie . . . it's tempting."

"How about a movie where you won't spend the entire time drooling over the cast? Like *Shrek*?"

"I don't know, Lucy, the donkey is pretty sexy . . ."

"I think that's illegal, Emily."

"Thinking about it isn't."

"I really hope you're joking."

"Don't worry, I am."

"The men in the white coats are going to come for you one day, you know."

"That sounds like fun."

"I didn't mean it like *that*."

"No, but I like my interpretation better."

"So are we going to watch *Shrek* or not?"

"Sure, but it always makes me get all mushy."

She rolls her eyes. "It's a kids' movie, Em."

"It's not really," I say. "It's multi-layered, you see. Like *The Simpsons*. You can watch it as a kid and think it's funny, and watch it when you're older and see other meanings in it. And *Shrek* is a very complex film, dealing with the isolation of the outcast."

"Mrs O'Shea must *love* you. Do you spout this type of crap in class?"

"When I'm awake."

"Ah, I see. I hear it's a good thing to stay conscious in school, now that you mention it. Something to do with learning."

"I think that's just a vicious rumour," I say.

She nods. "You're probably right." She switches on the TV and puts in the video. The door opens, and Lucy's mum sticks her head around it.

"Hi, Emily," she nods to me. "I'm making tea. Do you girls want any?"

"Sure, Mum," Lucy says.

"Emily?"

"Yeah, thanks," I say.

"Did you have a good time at the party last night?" she asks me.

"Yep, it was great."

"Missy here wasn't back until four in the morning," she says, her hand on Lucy's shoulder.

"That's disgraceful, Lucy," I say with a grin.

"You'll have to knock some sense into her, I think." She winks at me before going on.

Lucy turns to me and rolls her eyes. "How is it that my mother thinks you're a responsible person?"

I shrug. "I have no idea. My mother thinks you're the greatest thing since sliced bread."

"We really should swap," she muses.

But I know she doesn't mean it. Lucy and her mum get along really well. They go shopping together and they have long talks and share everything. I think it was the accident that brought them closer together. Before that, they were never really especially friendly.

Of course, before that, Lucy was out of control. Parents don't like that. They like their children to be following the rules and doing everything correctly. Step outside the lines and you're letting them down, disappointing them, making them wonder why they ever became parents in the first place.

CHAPTER THIRTY-FOUR

I leave Lucy's late in the evening. Her mum drops me home. I make a beeline for my room. I watch the rest of *Amelie* and consider whether setting a modern fairytale in Dublin would work – can anything filmed in Dublin be fairytale-like? The city looked pretty in *About Adam*, though, so I suppose you could make Dublin magical if you chose the right locations – before glancing at the Irish homework I'm supposed to do. If I were an organised person I'd do it now instead of putting it off until tomorrow night. Or I'd have done it on Thursday, when we were given it. However, I'm not organised, so I leave it on the desk and stare at the walls instead. There's a picture that Andrew took last summer of me, Barry and Lucy getting ready to go out one night.

"Barry, hold still," I ordered.

"It's hard to hold still when you're poking me in the eye," he said.

"I'm not poking you in the eye!" I protested. "The idea is that it goes around *the eye."*

"And I don't think you're doing a very good job of it," he told me.

"Well, we saw what happened when you tried to put eye-liner on yourself," I reminded him.

"Let us not speak of that day," Lucy giggled. She was painting his nails black.

He groaned. "Maybe I should just not look stupid."

"You don't look stupid," I told him. "You look sexy. If any-one looks stupid, it's Andrew."

"Hey!" Andrew protested.

"I think he looks great in PVC," Lucy said loyally.

"See?" he told us.

"Lucy's your girlfriend. She has to say that," I explained. "As your friend, I have to say – you look absolutely ridiculous."

"Look who's talking! You're making poor Barry wear make-up!"

"I'm not making him do anything. Besides, he looks good."

Andrew pretended to cough, muttering, "Drag queen!"

"I heard that," Barry said.

"Gender-bending is trendy," I said. "Look at Brian Molko. Early Brian Molko, of course. Sex on legs."

"She's got a point," Lucy said, blowing on Barry's nails.

I handed Barry a mirror. "What do you think?"

"Not bad," he smiled.

"Great."

"Smile!" Andrew said, holding up his camera.

"Oh, put it away," Lucy told him, hiding her face in her hands.

"Are you going to carry that everywhere this summer?" I
asked him.

"Pretty much," he shrugged.

I groaned.

"I'll make you a copy of the pictures," he promised.

*"Not much of a compensation for tormenting us for three
months,"* I told him.

"Oh, just smile for the camera," he said,

Barry and I struck a pose, and Andrew clicked.

So Lucy's to the side, trying to get out of the way of the
picture, and Barry and me are in our rock-star pose, all
made-up and dressed to kill. I remember that night.
We got hassled at the bus stop for looking weird, and
then we went into town where half the people there
were dressed "weirdly" and we were nothing special.
We had a good time. We went to a club that played
mostly what you'd call "alternative" music, I guess,
although I didn't think it was that alternative – just not
that much chart stuff.

We danced all night and were hot and sweaty at the
end of it. Going home I realised that I hadn't hooked
up with anyone or done anything out of the ordinary,
but I'd had a really great night out with my friends,
and that maybe that was all you really needed to be
happy.

CHAPTER THIRTY-FIVE

Lucy calls me up again on Sunday, which is unusual in that we can generally manage for more than twenty-four hours without talking. There's a part of me that suspects there's something she wants to tell me and meant to yesterday but couldn't, maybe to do with her and Andrew. Then again, she could just want to see me, but I have a feeling that isn't the case.

I look at the date and realise that it's two years to the day since the accident. I should have remembered. Everything happened at around the time of her sixteenth birthday, which fell on Holy Thursday, if I recall correctly. She was in the hospital two days later. I remember praying, even though I hadn't prayed properly in years. We pray in school, of course, but everyone sort of mutters the words and doesn't think about what they're saying.

Maybe that's it, maybe that's what she wants to talk about. Only she's never been that good with remembering dates. I had to remind her of when her anniversary with Andrew was.

I could be overreacting. She told me once that those few days in her life were blurred together for her now, and that she doesn't remember much of it, especially not what she was feeling. Maybe that's a good thing.

She comes over and we go to my room and sit on the

bed. She looks at the photo from my birthday party and says, "We all look so *young*."

"We are young," I remind her.

"Yeah, we are, aren't we? See, that's what I thought, we're still young, we have our whole lives ahead of us, don't we?" she says, sounding stressed.

I nod. "Does this have anything to do with Andrew and the whole being tied down thing?"

"Yeah," she sighs. "You know the way you said birthdays make you think about that sort of stuff?"

"Yeah?"

"Well, you know what else makes you think about that sort of stuff?"

"I have a feeling you're going to tell me."

"Marriage proposals."

I gape at her. *"What?"*

She nods. "I know! It's ridiculous, isn't it? He thinks it's time to take the next step in our relationship. We haven't even finished school and he's talking about getting married."

"When?"

"Oh, not soon, after college, I think, but he wants us to be engaged. To be able to say, yes, we're serious about each other and we're going to get married and have two point four kids and a dog and a goldfish and a dishwasher and a white picket fence."

"It's a bit scary," I say.

"A *bit*?" she shrieks. "I'm still revelling in the idea

that I can buy alcohol legally now and he's saying, 'Hey, let's plan out the rest of our lives.'"

"Haven't you talked about the future before, though?"

"Well, yeah, of course, but only vaguely. Like what we're going to do in college, and what jobs we'd like to have, and maybe where we'd like to live and what we'd call our kids, but I never really took it seriously, you know? I mean, you and Barry talk about what names you'd pick for your kids, and you don't mean it."

"Yeah, but we're not going out, and did you really think we'd inflict names like Ophelia and Horatio onto innocent children? We were trying to be all intellectual and . . . stuff."

"Still. You know what I mean. I never thought that Andrew was serious about it. But now he's all, 'Ooh, let's show everyone how much we really care about each other and how mature we are'."

"What did you tell him?"

"I said I'd think about it. What else could I say? It was after we got home on Friday night, and we were sitting in the car talking, and he brought it up. And I was going right, okay, what's going on, have I stepped into an alternate universe or something? He's really pissed off with me for not saying yes right away, though. He got all huffy. So I haven't spoken to him all weekend."

"Oh, Lucy, you should have said something yesterday. Me going on about Declan when you had this to think about."

"Yeah, but I was kind of hoping he'd call around and say he didn't really mean it and he's sorry for bringing it up. Now that I think about it, though, he's been hinting at this for a while. And it's so ridiculous, isn't it? I mean, I can't be engaged!"

"I know, I know." There's a sense of *déjà vu* about this, and I suddenly remember what comes next.

Chapter Thirty-Six

As I suspected, the girl in Boots didn't even blink when she saw that I was buying a pregnancy test. I found myself imagining what it would be like to be actually buying it for myself, though.

Lucy hadn't even had her sixteenth birthday yet and she might be having a baby. A child. She was going to be a mother and have to worry about whether her kid was wearing mittens and getting enough vitamins and all that stuff.

Back then I hadn't even thought about whether I wanted kids or not. It was never really an issue. Weird, that, considering that sex leads to babies and that while I was aware of the connection it had never really sunk in. I worried more about diseases, really. It's awful and politically incorrect and even statistically incorrect to say it now, but I'd always associated HIV with gay men, and the first guy I ever slept with had been with one or two guys before me. And I wasn't stupid; I knew that with all the stuff our crowd got up to, we were at risk for contracting pretty much everything there was. So I was always careful, and because of that, pregnancy had never been a real possibility. And I couldn't imagine what it would be like to have it be.

She was waiting for me to arrive. The door was open before I'd even walked up the driveway. I held up the bag, and she smiled.

"Oh, God, Emily, what would I do without you?" she said.

I asked if she'd told Andrew yet.

"I can't," she said. "I just can't face him right now."

"You'll have to eventually," I reminded her.

"I know, I know," she said, chewing on her hair distract-edly. She had it in two plaits and she looked so young. This couldn't be really happening, could it?

She took the bag from my hands and burst into tears. "Oh, God, Emily, I'm so scared."

"Shhh, shh," I soothed her, putting my arms around her. At that moment all I wanted to do was make everything okay. Never mind that we hadn't had a proper conversation in weeks or that I was only starting to get over her – this was my friend and I needed to do whatever I could, even though I felt completely helpless.

She dried her eyes and took out the test. "Well. Here we go."

It was positive. Forget about that little sliver of hope that we'd both had, that maybe it was all a mistake and she wasn't really pregnant. This was the real thing.

We sat on her bed, her talking, me listening.

"I don't know what I'm going to do," she said. "And Andrew – oh, God. I don't want to lose him, Em. I really don't. I don't know how I'd cope. Just the thought of it hurts me."

"You're not going to lose him," I reassured her. "He's crazy about you."

"It's ridiculous, isn't it?" she said. "This whole thing . . . I can't be pregnant. I just can't."

"I know," I said softly. "It doesn't feel real."

"Make it go away. Please. Make everything just be back to normal."

And then she kissed me.

CHAPTER THIRTY-SEVEN

"I just – oh, I don't know. Can't you just make it all go away? Make everything be normal again?" she smiles.

"What am I, your fairy godmother?" I laugh.

"You always seem to make things better," she says.

"Make me forget . . ."

"Forgetting isn't always a good idea," I say, but she's already incredibly close to me. How did that happen? And she's running her fingers along my lips and I know what's coming next, because we've been down this road before.

Lucy, you have to understand, is quite skilled in the art of kissing. Which is why I'm too distracted by this for a few minutes to even contemplate the idea of pushing her away.

It's not until the door swings open and Janet sticks her head in, asking, "Emily, do you know where –" that we stop.

"Do I know where what is?" I ask.

"What?" she says.

"Whatever you barged in here looking for," I remind her. "Speaking of which, don't you ever knock?"

"What, so you and your little *friend* can pretend that you're not up here *kissing?*" Never have I heard the word "kissing" used with so much disgust.

"No, because it's common courtesy!" I say.

"Don't try changing the subject, Emily," she says.

"And what exactly is the 'subject'?" I ask, exasperated.

"You! And *her!* Kissing!"

"Her name's Lucy," I remind Janet.

"Lucy?" Janet looks closer at her. "Does your *mother* know about this?"

"There's not really a 'this'," Lucy says.

"Oh, so what's going on here, then?" Janet demands. "Did you ever plan on telling us that you're batting for the other team, Emily?"

I roll my eyes at the euphemism. "There's nothing going on between me and Lucy," I say honestly. "Now, if you don't mind, tell me what you're looking for and then get the hell out of my room."

"I'm telling Mum," she says.

"You're *telling* on me?" I say in disbelief, and then shrug. "Fine. Tell her. I don't care."

Janet looks at me in frustration. Clearly this is not the right response. I should be begging her to keep my 'secret'. But I don't care. Honestly.

"Do you want me to go?" Lucy asks me quietly.

"No, it's okay. Stay," I say. "Janet, is there anything else you want?"

"No, I don't think so," she snaps, and storms out.

Lucy looks at me and raises her eyebrows. "Well. That was pleasant."

"She's just the greatest older sister, isn't she?" I say.

"Do you think she'll really tell your mum?" Lucy asks, looking worried.

I shrug. "No idea."

"Do you mind?"

"Not really, no," I say. "It's not like I'm trying to keep anything a secret. It's just – well, you know my parents. They don't have much interest in my life, and that's the way we all like it." I think about Lucy and her mum again, friends and not just mother and daughter.

"Sounds kind of lonely," she says softly.

I smile. "Nah. Not really."

"Still," she says, "you deserve, I don't know, parents who appreciate what an amazing person you are."

"Lucy, stop it," I say, because once again I know where she's going with this.

"It's the truth," she giggles, moving in to kiss me again.

"Lucy," I say more firmly. "No, stop."

"What's wrong?" she asks.

I don't even know where to begin with that one. It's the same thing that's always been wrong. The fact that she's never had any real feelings for me, no matter what she says.

CHAPTER THIRTY-EIGHT

I didn't know what to do or what to say, so I just went along with it, her kissing me, her taking off my T-shirt and telling me that I was such a good friend, and so beautiful, so very beautiful.

It reminded me of a dream, a dream that I'd had over and over again while sitting in school or lying in bed at night, only it was real. I was scared to blink in case I missed a single moment, in case it ended.

Lucy was the second girl I slept with, after Izzy. And I hadn't particularly cared about Izzy; that had just been an impulsive fling. It hadn't meant anything.

Lucy – Lucy meant something. Lucy meant something because I'd been crazy about her for months and because now, now she'd initiated it, and it had to mean something.

Her stomach was still flat. You could pretend that there wasn't really anything growing inside it, and that's what we did.

I didn't think about Andrew. Not then. Not until afterwards. I don't know if she did. I don't know if she'd cheated on him with anyone except me. She might well have. But I wanted to think I was special.

And she made me feel special. And loved, and peaceful, and happy.

And it meant absolutely nothing. To her.

CHAPTER THIRTY-NINE

"What's wrong?" she asks again.

"It's just – not this again, Lucy," I sigh.

"Oh, come on. It's just fun . . . you know that."

"No, it's not. It's not 'just fun'," I say. "It's you cheating on Andrew. It's me starting to think about all these feelings I used to have for you. It's not a good idea."

"I'm sorry," she says. "I didn't – I don't want to mess around with you, Em. You know I don't. I just thought that you didn't mind." She always thinks I don't mind.

"I wouldn't, usually," I say. "But it's *you.*"

"I hope you mean that in a good way," she giggles. "Not that I'm really repulsive or anything."

I smile. "You're not. Definitely not." Definitely, definitely, definitely not.

CHAPTER FORTY

After Lucy leaves, I go downstairs, where Janet, Mum and Dad are sitting, reading various sections of *The Sunday Times*. Mum reads the fashion stuff, Dad the sports and business stuff, and Janet reads the political stuff.

"Is Lucy gone?" Mum asks.

"Yeah," I nod, wondering what's coming next.

But that's all, it seems. I pick up *The Funday Times* and leave the room.

Sunday afternoons are always depressing. It's the weekend, but you know that the weekend is coming to an end, and that there were things you meant to do but didn't, and that when you wake up the next morning you have a whole week of school ahead of you.

So I call Barry, and we babble on for a while before Dad tells me to get off the phone because he needs to make a call, and no, he doesn't intend on using his mobile when he has a perfectly good land-line, and that I really don't need to be on the phone for someone who lives nearby and who I saw yesterday.

Clearly he doesn't understand that yes, I do need to talk to Barry, but arguing with him is pointless. He thinks I'm one of those teenagers who like talking on the phone for the sake of talking. I wonder what it's like to be an adult and have grown-up phone conversations. They always seem so dull. I mean, sometimes there's a bit of gossip, but mostly – it's so boring and routine. I guess they must think that we're a melodramatic bunch, turning everything into a life-or-death situation – but I think I prefer being dramatic to being bland.

Dad is now on the phone making small talk to my Auntie Mary. It is extraordinarily dull. I mean, what Barry and I were talking about – reliving Lucy's party – was much more interesting. We were deciding on who the most attractive people there were, and agreed on Natasha and Steven. Lucy had the best outfit and Philip had the worst. Not that he looked unattractive, but he could have made more of an effort. And apparently Jean and Natasha had a fight because Jean was –

allegedly – all over Philip on the way home in the taxi.

Ah, gossip. It's just lovely. I mean, people say it's a bad thing to gossip, but it's so much fun. I don't go in for the bitching, much, just discussing stuff. Unless of course it's about Declan and I'm in a crappy mood.

But I don't want to think about Declan, because I'll just get annoyed. He'll get over this, I'm sure, and we can go back to being friends, and in the meantime I'm going to sit back and relax and enjoy the rest of my weekend.

CHAPTER FORTY-ONE

Everyone hates Mondays apart from my Irish teacher, who is cheerful and enthusiastic and says things like, "Look, I know you're all tired after the weekend, but we still have work to do!" That would actually mean something if she herself was tired, cranky and wanting to be anywhere but school, like normal people are on Monday mornings. But no, she's chirpy and yammering on about the poetry and what it really means.

I find it hard enough to write about what poetry in English really means. I can't believe they expect us to be able to do that in Irish, too. I whisper to Sarah about Lucy's party instead. I wonder if Sarah knows that she and Shane weren't invited because Shane and Lucy haven't been on very good terms ever since they had a little fling last Christmas, and Andrew still hates Shane for it. It's a good thing they're not in the same year at school; bad enough that they're in the same building. Barry told me they almost got into a fight one day at lunch.

Lucy and Shane are both such flirts, I don't know why it surprised anyone. Andrew wasn't there and she needed someone, basically. He forgave her, though. Of course, he did. They're madly in love, despite it all.

Sometimes – when we're not all making fun of how we just know they're going to spend the rest of their lives together and live happily ever after and how sickening it all is – I think we all wish that we had something like that.

Other times I'm sensible. Like Barry says, I'm commitment-phobic. He can hardly talk, though. The only relationship he's ever had that comes close to being remotely serious is what he had with Jeremy. I guess that was serious, actually. I mean, he was throwing around words like 'soul mate' and 'fate', although he'd kill me if I ever repeated those things to anyone. But apart from that, he's always been restless, needing to move on after a certain amount of time.

It's the best way to be, isn't it? Not to be tied down when you're a teenager? I mean, you have the rest of your life to settle down with someone and be dull and grown up and respectable.

Would I settle down with Abi? Yeah, I suppose I

would. If only. We would live in an apartment in town and it would be terribly stylish. She would be working at a magazine or a publisher or something and I would be – well, I don't know what I'd be doing. Maybe making movies. I wish. Probably something else, something less exciting. We would go out to clubs and party all night and arrive home at four in the morning and fall into bed together.

It'd be perfect, an idyllic life. I wonder how long it would take for me to get bored with it.

CHAPTER FORTY-TWO

Hugh and I being together made sense to everyone. Between the fact that we'd known each other for such a long time and the fact that we were going around saying that we'd always known that there was something more than friendship between us, everyone was convinced that we were going to last forever.

Except Barry, who was subjected to my fits of melodrama and angst about why Hugh was being so very reserved with me as far as sex was concerned. I accepted his explanation that Hugh was just nervous, but it was getting to me. I wasn't used to things moving slowly, and considering that we had been able to skip the getting-to-know-each-other phase, it seemed as if we were going to be stuck in the same place forever, with his hands firmly planted on my waist and never wandering anywhere else.

We slept together for the first time two weeks before we broke up. I think he'd had a conversation with Shane and that had spurred him into action, the realisation that he had a girlfriend who was not going to tell him that she wanted to wait until she had a ring on her finger or talk about needing more time, someone who didn't think it was a big deal.

There were quite a few people from school at Sarah's party. I was trying to avoid Hugh, who was in let's-talk-about-nothing-else-but-music mode, and so I was talking to Christine from my maths class. I looked over at Hugh and realised he wasn't missing me, busy as he was talking to a few of his friends. There was Shane, and a blonde girl who I'd been introduced to before but whose name escaped me, and a redhead . . . who I hadn't seen before.

I must have seen her before, I thought. She was one of Sarah's friends, wasn't she? But I'd never seen her outside of school before, not wearing the uniform. Don't stare, I told myself, and tried to concentrate on what Christine was saying.

He came over to me after a while, leaving his group and putting his arms around me. "You want to go?" he asked.

"Yeah," I said. I was getting sleepy and I could feel a headache coming on. I hadn't been drinking much. I thought the headache was probably from listening to Christine for so

long. She was a lovely girl, but honestly, she never stopped talking.

We walked to my house and I said goodnight at the front door, looking forward to crawling into my bed and pulling the covers over my head.

He took my hand and said, "Aren't you going to invite me in?"

I shrugged. "Okay, if you want to, come in for a while . . ."

The house was dark. The parents were asleep, clearly. I switched on the lights downstairs and asked him if he wanted tea or coffee.

"Just you," he said.

"That's so corny," I laughed.

He pulled me down onto the couch and started kissing me. My heart wasn't in it. I kept thinking about the girl at the party and about how my head was really aching and how I just wanted to go to sleep.

It was when he started unzipping my trousers that I said, "Hugh, can't we do this some other time? I'm really tired."

He didn't listen to me.

"Hugh," I said firmly, sitting up and pulling my trousers up, "I'm tired. I don't want to do this now, okay?"

"You don't really mean that," he said.

I rolled my eyes. "Yeah, I do. That's why I'm saying it. I'll see you tomorrow, okay?"

"You're just like all the rest of them," he told me.

"Excuse me?"

"I mean, were you just playing with me all this time?" he demanded. "Making me believe that this is what you wanted, and then changing your mind about it? I thought you were better than that. I thought I knew you."

"Don't give me this crap, Hugh," I said. "You do know me, well enough to know that you can't manipulate me like this."

"Oh, you're talking about manipulation?"

"Just go. Please. We can discuss this some other time."

"Forget it, Emily. You're not who I thought you were. You're just another tease."

"I didn't mean to –" I began, feeling the tears in my eyes. Maybe he was right. I had led him on, after all, and wasn't it completely hypocritical of me to turn around now and say that I didn't want the very thing that I'd been asking for since the moment we started going out?

"Oh, you didn't 'mean to'!" he said in disgust.

"Hugh, stop it," I said.

He was about to leave. It wasn't until he opened the front door that I called after him. I knew I had to make things better, make up for what I'd done. So I went along with his original plan, and we pretended we'd never fought.

But things were different after that, even though we wanted to pretend that they weren't. Something had disappeared, the magical thing that had made our relationship work. So he turned his attentions to Fiona, and I turned mine to Abi, and when we broke up, we weren't shocked, even though everyone else was.

I don't know what to say about what happened that night. I cried, you see, after he left. I didn't know why I was crying. Maybe it was because I really hadn't wanted to sleep with him that night, or maybe it was because I'd let myself be manipulated, or maybe it was because I was weak and I was a tease and a tramp and I knew that I deserved it.

CHAPTER FORTY-THREE

He was still *mine*, though. I think that's the part that upset me. That he was supposed to be my boyfriend and that he decided that I wasn't good enough anymore. What an asshole! It's guys like him that make me want to exterminate the entire male species. (And thoughts like those that get me a reputation for being a man-hater, but I digress.)

I'm over it, like I said. I'm not the type to sit around moping over an ex, and in retrospect it was the best thing that could have happened. We're good at being friends, even though we haven't been *real* friends in a while. It's been a casual, off-hand sort of thing ever since we broke up. It'll take a while for things to get back to normal, I suppose.

But it always does, doesn't it? It's what's happening with Declan right now. I really must call him sometime this week and get everything sorted out. I don't want this becoming a big deal.

It isn't. It shouldn't be.

CHAPTER FORTY-FOUR

Monday seems to last forever. I am incredibly relieved to get home, and even more relieved that it's a Janet-free environment at the moment.

I head for the TV, of course, and debate which DVD to watch. I find myself wondering if my parents ever look at my collection. If Janet had ever examined it closely, she wouldn't have been so surprised at seeing me kissing Lucy.

I'm annoyed about that, I think. Not intensely annoyed, but irritated that she's barged into my private life and made judgements based on five seconds. My friendship, or relationship, or whatever you want to call it, with Lucy, is something rather complicated. And Janet has no idea. She just makes assumptions.

I hate her for intruding on this part of my life, the part of my life that I keep for just me and my friends, the part I don't want my family knowing about, and it's not out of any sense of shame or fear, but the fact that they don't know who I am, the sort of person that I am, and that we're just people who live in the same house and are bound by blood but not by anything that really matters.

I'm moving out as soon as I can, not because I hate them – I don't – but because I need my own space. I need to have my own life, and right now it feels like I can't have that here.

I want that stylish apartment in town where I will live with someone I care about. Since Abi's out of the question, realistically speaking, I'd probably end up sharing with Barry. I imagine living with him. We'd always be laughing at something. I'd come home from a long hard day at work and he'd give me a back massage. Then I'd give him one – because he would have had a tough day too – and then we'd –

No. I'm not going down that route. Roisín and the others must be getting to me with their 'spark' nonsense.

CHAPTER FORTY-FIVE

I spend Tuesday lunch-time talking to Lucy about Andrew's proposal.

"I called him yesterday," she says. "He said he didn't understand why I wasn't excited about this."

I sigh. "He's being a little unreasonable, isn't he? I mean, you're *eighteen*."

"I tried telling him that. He says that he's ready to commit, and that he doesn't get why I'm not willing to.

I think I'm going to end it."

"End it?" I say fearfully. Being friends with Declan has made me paranoid about people saying things like that.

"Break up with him," she elaborates, and I breathe a sigh of relief.

"Do you mean it?" I ask.

She nods. "This isn't just going to go away, you know? I need to deal with it, and I think the only way I can is by telling him I can't be involved with him any more."

"But it's Andrew. I mean – you're mad about him, right?"

"Of course," she says, "but what else can I do? So I'm going to talk to him today after school."

"There has to be a better way of dealing with this than dumping him, Lucy," I say. I'm still stunned at the idea that the perfect couple are going to be no more. "I mean, you've had fights before, but you've always stayed together."

She looks at me in an almost condescending manner. "Emily, I know you don't understand this. But some-day you will."

Make that an *extremely* condescending manner.

"Okay," I say. "Call me later if you need someone to talk to, okay?"

She nods. "Okay. Thanks."

She goes back to her classroom and I go into the

bathroom where I take out my phone and call Andrew.

"Heya. We need to talk."

CHAPTER FORTY-SIX

Once again I am leaving school early in an attempt to sort out someone else's life. I meet up with Andrew outside his school just before his lunch-time is over. He has a study period after lunch he can get away with missing. I have forty minutes to talk some sense into him.

We are sitting underneath the trees beside their basketball court, amid cigarette butts and empty crisp packets. I say, "Honestly, Andrew, what were you *thinking*, proposing to Lucy?"

He looks embarrassed. "I thought it'd be romantic. Besides – you know I'm . . ."

"Madly in love with her," I supply.

"Yeah," he grins. "I wanted to show her that, because sometimes I don't think she gets it. I mean, everyone's always going on about how cute and sweet we are and how we're going to get married eventually – and by everyone I mean mostly you," he adds, and I laugh. "And we don't really talk about it, but sometimes we're like, we should just go and get married to shut everyone up. And I started thinking, well, she's the one person I really want to spend the rest of my life with – so what's the point in waiting?"

I nod. "Yeah. I see your point."

"Of course, it turns out that she clearly doesn't feel the same way," he says bitterly, "and that she's basically just been wasting time with me for the last two years."

"It's not like that."

"It feels like it."

"Andrew, she loves you. You *know* she loves you. Her eyes light up whenever you're around and she can't stand being separated from you for more than a day . . ."

"Although she does seem to manage. How many times has she cheated on me?"

I sigh. He's got a point. "A few," I admit.

"How many times with you, even?" he asks. "I mean, she just does whatever the hell she feels like. I should have known she wouldn't say yes."

"She's scared," I say.

"Of me?"

"Of committing herself. Of saying to someone, 'Yes, I love you, completely and utterly, and I want to spend the rest of my life with you, and be faithful to you'. It's tough. It's tough enough for people in their twenties and thirties to say it, and she's eighteen, Andrew. She's worried about whether she's going to get the points to do what she wants in college. She doesn't need to be thinking about this stuff right now, and neither do you."

"Emily, you really don't get it –"

"I am *sick* of being told that I don't 'get it'. What I 'get' is that two people I really care about are going to fight about something completely *ridiculous* and destroy the most amazing relationship I've ever seen. And I don't want to see that."

"You're really one to be talking about destroying relationships, aren't you?" he asks.

"What's that supposed to mean?" I ask, confused. "Hugh was the one who ended it with me, remember?" Unless – unless Hugh has been telling people about the night after Sarah's party, and how I led him on and played games, and Andrew sees his point of view. I start to feel slightly sick. Stupid Hugh, stupid Hugh – I'm angry. Of course I'm angry. I'm angry that he made me feel guilty about it, that's what. And yes I can forgive him, and yes I can still be friends with him, but I will never forget, and it will never happen again. I will never let myself be manipulated like that ever again, by anyone.

Andrew is staring at me. "Not Hugh."

I'm confused. Only – oh, no, don't tell me he's going to blame me for ruining his relationship with Lucy. "What are you talking about, then?" I ask. Part of me needs to know, and the other part of me really doesn't want to.

He continues staring. "Emily, *think* for a second. What have you done recently which has upset the guy that is absolutely crazy about you?"

"You mean Declan? He'll get over the fact that I don't want a long-term thing," I say.

He smacks his head against his forehead. "Barry, Emily!"

"What about Barry?"

He looks like he wants to scream. "Well, he's not exactly thrilled about you and Declan, is he?"

"No, but – it's not because he's in *love* with me or anything, Andrew," I say, finally understanding what he's trying to tell me.

"What makes you so sure?"

"Because he'd tell me," I say.

"It's not always easy to tell people how you feel," he says.

"Yeah, but if you *know* them . . ."

"It's even harder." He sighs. "I mean, I told Lucy how I felt, and now I have this really, really expensive engagement ring sitting at home gathering dust and a 'serious talk' after school."

"Tell her you're willing to wait. That you're sorry for rushing her into this and that on consideration, it's too early to think about marriage."

"Yeah, but –"

"Unless of course you want to keep insisting that she should be ready, and lose her," I say.

"I'll talk to her. I just wish she was willing to show people how much she cares about me."

"She's got 'Lucy loves Andrew' written over all her books at school," I say.

"That's not the same," he says, but laughs.

"Yeah, I know. It's not grown-up enough, is it? But she's *not*. She's only just turned eighteen. Look, I know we all like playing at being grown-ups. We talk about politics and issues and relationships and all that stuff – but we're not grown up. Not yet."

"Speak for yourself," he says, and smiles. "Thanks."

"No problem," I say.

CHAPTER FORTY-SEVEN

Unsurprisingly enough, I find myself thinking about what Andrew said as I walk home. Everything's swirling around in my head and none of it makes any sense. I mean – Barry. And – liking me. And – no. It's ridiculous. Andrew doesn't know what he's talking about.

Because no one really knows what they're talking about when it comes to me and Barry. Everyone thinks they've got us figured out, everyone thinks that we're secretly lusting after each other and that there's a 'spark' between us – and they don't have a clue.

I mean, of course he's attractive. But the fact that I

can see this doesn't mean that I'm attracted *to* him. There's a difference.

If we liked each other we'd have done something about it at this stage. We're hardly shy. Of course, we'd be terrible in a relationship. It'd never last. We'd be cheating on each other within a week. It would never work out between us.

Only, you know, it might. We could have a perfect future together in that stylish apartment with the wide-screen TV and modern art and double bed. No, I need to get my mind out of the gutter.

It really likes it there, though.

What *is* this? I mean, suddenly I'm thinking about Barry in a new light, and the guy who has been my best friend for years is now suddenly potential boyfriend material. It makes no sense. I can't believe I'm letting everyone else's opinions get to me like this. Because that must be it. There's no other logical explanation.

CHAPTER FORTY-EIGHT

Lucy still hasn't called by eight o'clock, so I end up ringing her to see what happened. She sounds happy and giggly when she answers. "Hey, Em!"

"Heya. You sound pretty cheerful."

"I am indeed. I was just about to call you, actually. I have some *wonderful* news for you."

Wonderful news? That she's not breaking up with Andrew, I hope.

"I'm engaged!" she sings.

My mouth drops open. And then I just laugh. I completely crack up. "You're insane," I splutter.

She's laughing almost as hard as I am. "I know. But – it seems like the right thing to do."

"Oh, Lucy. What happened?"

"He went all mushy and romantic on me," she says.

I can hear him in the background saying, "Oh, I did not. Shut up."

"And that made you change your mind?" I say incredulously.

"I cried," she admits. "You know I love him – and I know what I'm doing. I want to do this. I didn't at first, but – I don't know, I guess it gets to a certain point where you have to stop being a kid, right?"

"Right," I say, still a little in shock at this new Lucy. I mean, I was there for the change from irresponsible Lucy to hardworking student Lucy, but ready-to-commit Lucy is something I've never seen before.

"You think I'm crazy, don't you?" she says, sounding somewhat hurt.

"No! No," I reassure her. (Yes.) "It's kind of – unexpected – but I am really happy for you. For both of you." And I mean it. Really. I mean, there's this lump in my throat. That must mean I'm sincere, right?

"That means a lot, sweetie," she says.

119

"I have to go," I say. "I'll talk to you soon, okay?"

"Okay," she says, and I hang up.

And then I, rather dramatically, burst into tears.

Chapter Forty-Nine

Well, what did I expect? I should have seen this coming, despite Lucy's protests that she wasn't serious about her relationship with Andrew. I've always known she was in love with him, right? I've always known that she was going to spend the rest of her life with him.

Of course, I wasn't convinced at the beginning. But then, after the accident . . . I saw how much he cared. I thought maybe it was just that he felt responsible, but I saw the way Lucy pleaded with him not to feel guilty, that she was equally to blame, if not more so.

They took Andrew's brother's motorbike for a ride. It was Lucy's idea. She's one of those people who love wind in their hair and anything that goes fast. She goes crazy over rides at amusement parks, never holding on to the safety bars, laughing at people who look worried as she leans over the side or dangles upside-down.

What Lucy's intention that night was is anyone's guess. Andrew knows, I'm sure. I don't. I was afraid to ask. What I do know is that it was she who convinced him to borrow his brother's bike, and she was the one who kept encouraging him to go faster and faster, and then yelled at him to swerve. She said she saw something, a cat or a dog on the road. He said he didn't see anything, but it was dark. He swerved. The bike skidded. They crashed.

They were both thrown off the bike. A car passing by saw the whole thing, and the driver called an ambulance.

It was one a.m. on Saturday morning. I didn't hear about it until the early afternoon, when Lucy's mother called me.

They let Andrew out of hospital the next day. They kept Lucy in. I remember being there, at the hospital, with him and Lucy's family and one or two of our friends.

He wanted a cigarette, so we went outside. I watched him light up and inhale, then exhale. His hands were shaking.

"They all blame me, you know," he said.

"It wasn't your fault," I said. "It was an accident, remember?"

He shook his head. "It was my fault. I shouldn't have been drinking."

"You were drinking?" I asked.

He nodded. "I shouldn't have let her —"

"Let her what?"

"Let her talk me into taking the bike."

I wondered if she'd told him about the baby.

She hadn't. She did, later, when she came home. She had a sprained wrist, but thankfully no brain damage – and she wasn't pregnant any more.

She cried a bit but mostly she just set about getting her life in order. I told her to talk to Andrew, tell him that it wasn't his fault, and she did.

I don't know whether he believed her or not, but they were even closer than they had been after that.

And no matter what happened after that, no one could possibly come between them.

CHAPTER FIFTY

And now they're engaged, they're going to be married, she's going to wear a white dress and walk up the aisle and say "I do".

And I'm crying. I don't know why. Is it because I'm happy for them? No. I care about them, but this – I'm not sure whether I'm happy about it or not.

The phone is ringing. I wonder if it's Lucy again. Someone picks up. Dad calls, "Emily, it's for you."

Great. I sniff and rub at my eyes and pick up the phone. "Hello?"

"Heya." It's Barry. "Are you okay?"

"Yeah, I'm fine," I say. "Um. I think."

"Lucy said she called you to tell you the news," he continues.

"Ah, yes. Did she call you?"

"Yep." He pauses. "So – what do you think?"

"I think they're insane, personally, and either they'll go through with it and end up divorced within a year, or else they'll eventually come to their senses. Or else they'll live happily ever after and have a perfect little happy romantic life and . . . wow, do I sound bitter?"

"Are you?"

"Yes. No. I don't know."

"That's what I love about you, Em, your decisiveness," he teases.

"I want that," I say in a little voice.

He's confused. "Decisiveness?"

"No. The happily ever after part. I want that. I want what they have. I mean, they're so happy together. They really love each other, you know? And I think it's worse that it's Lucy and that she's, I don't know, permanently off-limits now."

"I thought you were over Lucy," he says.

"I was. I am. I thought I was." I don't *know* any more. I thought I got over her a long time ago. But her relationship with Andrew has never exactly stopped her from flirting with me – or anyone else for that matter – or going further than that.

I never had *closure*, I suppose. *Closure* is what Americans talk about the whole time, an idea that's infiltrating our minds too as we get used to all this trendy psychobabble. (This is something I picked up during my pretentious phase.) You need to say good-bye to a certain area of your life before you can move on and develop your full potential as a human being and get in touch with your inner child and all that nonsense.

And now closure has been forced upon me, in the form of one of my dearest friends and ex-crush signing her life away. I mean, what is she thinking? I thought I'd talked him out of this whole marriage thing. Apparently not.

"Maybe it's just that this is sort of final," Barry suggests.

"Yeah," I say, "that's probably it. What do you think about it?"

"I can't see Lucy as the faithful wife type, somehow," he says. "I don't see Andrew loving married life either."

"Really? He seems pretty keen on the idea."

"Yeah, but I don't think that'll last. I think he'll end up regretting getting himself into this situation after a while."

"Ah, of course. What a typically male attitude," I tease.

"Of course! We don't want to commit. We're designed to be as promiscuous as possible."

"While the women stay at home and have the babies, right?"

"And do the cooking and the cleaning."

"Ah, yes."

"And the washing and the ironing."

"Naturally. Remind me never to marry you."

"Oh, Emily, you wound me."

"You can take it."

"True."

"Talk to you tomorrow?"

"Yeah. See ya."

"Bye."

Chapter Fifty-One

It's only Wednesday and it feels like it should be the weekend. I'd be incredibly grateful if any higher power out there would make time move that little bit quicker so that it can be Friday night and I can curl up in bed and avoid the world for a few days.

Well, that's a tad dramatic. I suppose it's not that bad. All the same, I'd prefer to be at home than sitting in school thinking about Lucy-and-Andrew, Andrew-and-Lucy, and everything that comes with it.

I don't know what's going on here, and it's all terribly confusing. I thought things were nice and simple. You know, being vaguely annoyed but amused about the Hugh situation, having tension with Declan, having a crush on Abi, and rolling my eyes at people going on about that 'spark'.

And now all of a sudden Abi has faded into the background and while I still think she's a perfectly lovely girl and I want to keep an eye on her in case she does anything stupid, I'm not fantasising about her in a romantic way.

Roisín said to me, when I first told her I liked Abi, that she thought it was a rebound thing, considering things had just ended between me and Hugh. It's easy to see these things from a distance, I suppose – when it's you, you think that you know what's best and what's real.

And I'm thinking about Lucy, who is part of my past, who is a dear friend but who is in no way a romantic figure in my life any more, and it's – it's a mess.

My past is a list of experiences. Not mistakes – none of them were – but experiences, and if I had the chance to go back and change something, I wouldn't. I wouldn't be me otherwise, and I *like* me.

But I do wish that the past would just stay put and stop waving its hand at me saying, "I feel sort of un-resolved. Here, go and question your feelings all over again, there's a good girl." It's very inconsiderate of it.

I'll probably be seeing Barry tonight. He cheered me up yesterday; he'll help me sort things out in my head.

I really don't know what I'd do without him.

And that then brings up another issue, namely the idea that everyone has been right all along and that we're destined to end up together. I'm not sure if they are yet, but it's looking like a maybe at the moment.

Although I mustn't be thinking clearly at the moment, since everything seems so chaotic right now, so I won't mention this to him. I don't want to mess up our friendship. I can't.

Chapter Fifty-Two

"I thought you might be interested in this," Roisín says to me at lunch-time, handing me a thin brochure.

We're alone in the classroom; everyone else is either outside or has gone home. I am curious as to what it is that I might be interested in.

Maybe Barry's been talking to her and she's brought me a leaflet on "How To Deal With Your First Lesbian Crush Getting Married" or something along those lines. Maybe it has handy tips on how to not start screaming during that "if anyone knows why these two should not be joined in holy matrimony" part of the wedding, and how to make a speech that isn't bitter.

A speech. What if she wants me to be the maid of honour? She always said that I would be, at her wedding, even though neither of us thought she'd have to make a decision quite so soon.

The brochure does not, in fact, have anything to do with solving the chaos in my life. It's about a summer course for "young film-makers".

"I'm not a young film-maker," I point out, looking at the cover.

"You don't have to have experience," she says. "You just have to be interested, and you are. It sounds like your sort of thing."

"Yeah, but – " I flip through it, but only half-heartedly. My mind's still on Lucy and Barry and Declan. It does look sort of interesting, I suppose, but it'd mean I'd miss out on part of my summer. I wanted to spend this summer relaxing and not doing anything. Having to take part in something for several weeks doesn't quite count as 'doing nothing'.

So maybe I do want to make movies or be involved with them in some way when I'm older, but I hate the idea that you have to go to school for everything, rather than learn from your life experience. School doesn't teach you about life. A summer course isn't going to change my career prospects.

"But what?" she asks.

"Nothing," I say, and try to smile.

"Is something going on?"

I contemplate telling her everything, but I'm not sure where I'd begin. I'm grateful when the door swings open and a group of girls walk in, munching on popcorn. The decision has been made for me. I'm never sure how comfortable she is with me talking seriously about Lucy and girls in general, anyway.

128

"Not really," I say, and then add, "I just can't wait for it to be summer." At least that much is true.

CHAPTER FIFTY-THREE

"So what are we watching tonight, oh wise one?" he asks.

"Depends. What are you in the mood for?"

"Porn," he kids. Or perhaps he's serious.

"I don't have porn, Barry," I remind him.

"Yeah, you do, that Spanish one with all the sex."

"Mexican. And it's *artistic.*"

"Sure, sure."

"It is!"

"Whatever you say," he says innocently. He looks through the collection. "*Boys and Girls?* Isn't that a bit too low-brow for you, Emily?"

"Are you forgetting I also own *Crossroads*? And anyway, it's got two girls kissing in it, which makes up for a lot."

"I knew there had to be a reason you had such a typical romantic comedy in here."

"Are you implying that I couldn't just own a typical romantic comedy because I liked it?" I tease.

He considers this. "Yeah, pretty much. I mean, it's a story about two really great friends who end up falling in love and living happily ever after. Not your sort of thing, is it?"

I stare at him for a moment. "Maybe it's exactly my sort of thing," I say.

"Oh, really?" he says, raising an eyebrow.

"Really," I say, and we're doing this thing where we're inching towards each other, and then I laugh. "Barry, we have to stop doing this."

"What? Flirting?"

"No, using a Freddie Prinze Jr movie as a not-so-subtle metaphor for whatever's going on with us."

He grins. "Hey, you're the one who has it on DVD. There's got to be a reason for that."

"I told you. It's the kiss."

"That's the only reason?" he smiles.

"Absolutely," I nod. And now we're inching again. I know where this is going. And, you know, I think I like it. Maybe it's crazy and insane, but I like it, and my instincts are telling me that this is definitely the right thing to do.

CHAPTER FIFTY-FOUR

"Guess what I did last night?" I sing-song to Roisín on Thursday morning.

"Declared your undying love for Barry?" she teases.

I shrug. "Close enough."

The look on her face is priceless. I've been giggling to

myself with delight all morning at the thought of seeing this look. It's classic disbelief, tinged with a bit of shock and a healthy dose of I-told-you-so.

"Are you serious?" she splutters.

I nod. "Yep."

"Emily!" she shrieks, causing a couple of other girls sitting in the classroom to look at us strangely. "I can't believe it!"

I grin. I love having good news like this. "Yeah. He was over last night, we were just talking, and then – then . . . "

"Then you propositioned him," she smiles.

"Nope. I kissed him. Or he kissed me. There was a kiss, anyway. And then there was more kissing. And then we said goodnight. And we were all happy and smiley and stuff. Quite sickening, actually."

"I can imagine. But – you kissed him? And that's all? That seems terribly chaste for you, Em."

"What's that supposed to mean?" I ask, but I know what she means.

"You just tend to move fast, that's all," she says. "Not that it's a bad thing, but –"

"Nah, you're right. But this is different. Me and Barry – aaagh! I can't believe it." I really can't. It's me and Barry. Me and Barry! And yet it seems to make so much sense, when you think about it. We're like two halves of the same coin, coming together to form a perfect whole.

Oh, here we go again with the romantic babbling. It feels familiar. But this isn't like it was with Hugh. This is completely different. I feel it.

CHAPTER FIFTY-FIVE

At break-time Roisín, me, and a few others are sitting around chatting when she brings up the topic of Barry again.

"Barry, as in your friend Barry?" Christine asks.

"Yeah, him," I say.

"Emily's decided she's madly in love with him," Roisín adds.

I watch their reactions. They look surprised. More than that, they look disbelieving. They look as if they want to say, "Right, Emily, you're not fooling us. We all know you're a big mad dyke, so stop pretending."

Maybe I'm overreacting. But their *looks* . . . And now we have the feigned interest.

"Is he good-looking?" Maria asks.

"Very," I say, but I watch her. I watch the patronising smile. I watch the way they seem to act as though they're playing parts in a play, pretending right along with me.

Truth be told, it's been going on for a while now. The averted eyes (because eye contact could be interpreted as being *interested*, and that'd be a disaster of colossal proportions), the awkwardness whenever I'm the only other person in the room.

They're right in one way, I guess. I'm pretending, but it's not about pretending to be interested in guys, it's about pretending that I don't care.

And I find myself needing to leave. Right now. I know it's going to look suspicious and probably just give them more to gossip about, but I can't stand being around them any more.

A couple of weeks ago, these girls were my friends. I mean, we weren't close, not like me and Roisín or me and Barry or even me and Abi, but we were friends. And now everything's different, and I don't know whether I like it or not. I didn't get a choice in the matter. In some ways I'm glad about this – taking the burden off my shoulders, I guess – but in other ways I resent it.

It's my life. Not theirs. How dare they sit there and judge me and whisper about how they suspected all along how I wasn't "normal"? Whisper about Abi when she walks in, whisper whenever I'm talking privately to another girl, whisper, whisper, whisper. I am sick of it, so incredibly sick and tired of it all.

I hide in the bathroom. Bathrooms are good for this sort of thing, this kind of emotional upheaval. I wonder how many girls have leaned against this cold tiled wall and tried not to cry.

"Emily? You in here?" Roisín calls.

I unlock the door and walk out, staring at myself in the mirror. Girl. Seventeen years old. Brunette, for the moment. Semi-attractive. Wearing school uniform. Upset. Angry. Scared.

"You okay?" she asks softly.

I want to say something profound and meaningful, explain the way I'm feeling. Instead I just burst into tears. I'm such a girl.

"I'd never make a good lesbian," I sniffle.

Roisín looks at me, puzzled.

"I'm not butch enough," I elaborate, with half a smile.

She giggles. "So you're buying into the stereotypes now?"

I shrug. "Everyone else seems to be."

"So what are you, then?"

"The resident bisexual slut, clearly," I say.

"You sound bitter," she says quietly.

"Oh, you think? I *hate* this school. I hate the way they make me *question* myself over and over and *think* about all this stuff and turn it into a big deal. I hate the way they look at me, and I hate the way they think they know everything about me. So, yeah, I'm bitter." And the tears are starting up again.

"Oh, sweetie," she says, giving me a hug. "Ignore them, okay? They're not important."

"I hate them," I sniffle.

"You never cared what they thought about you before," she reminds me gently.

"That was different," I say. That was before my personal life became a topic of classroom gossip. It's easy to be indifferent when everything's going okay.

Roisín pauses. "You're still you," she says eventually. "And the Emily I know does her own thing and doesn't worry about what everyone else is going to say."

I smile. I love her so much at this moment for that. And I start to dry my eyes.

Chapter Fifty-Six

I get home on Thursday and stare at the photos on the wall, grinning like an idiot whenever I see one with me and Barry. How could I not have seen it before? We make the perfect couple.

Everyone else has been seeing it for ages, of course. It's so obvious to them. I can't *believe* it's taken me so long to realise this.

I sit on the bed and sigh. He's probably got a lot of homework to do tonight. I won't see him.

There's a message on my phone. Heart pounding. It's from him. I resist the urge to squeal in delight.

I am so very giddily happily in love and I adore it. This is the sort of 'sickening' behaviour that Roisín teases me about, but I don't care. I'm *happy*.

I go over to his house after dinner and we hang out in his room, just talking at first, and then he says, "So . . ."

And I say, "So . . ."

We laugh.

"About yesterday," I say, and he looks worried.

"Look, if you – " he begins.

"I don't regret it," I reassure him quickly. "And I'm glad it happened."

"Really?" he smiles. (He is truly adorable when he smiles. It's so cute!)

"Really," I say, and kiss him.

We are still kissing – and going no further, may I add – when his mother knocks on the door and asks us if we'd like anything to drink.

She seems surprised, but in a good way, to see me and Barry jump apart, embarrassed. He never told her about Jeremy, but I think she must have suspected. For months, they spent all their time together, and after they broke up he stayed in his room, miserable, for a week. How can parents _not_ notice things like that? How can they not make the connection? She must have known something was going on.

Parents are experts at the game of denial, I suppose. If they don't want to see something . . . it doesn't exist for them.

I want to call her on that almost-relieved look and tell her that Barry would probably be better off with

Jeremy, that I'm really not the sort of girl that anyone should go out with. I want to ask her why she thinks it's automatically better for him to be with a girl than a boy.

I'm jumping to conclusions, I realise, and reading too much into the situation. The world isn't out to get us.

Did I just say 'us'? 'Us', as in the lesbian-gay-bisexual-transgendered-queer community? 'Us', as in me and *them*?

As in me, the girl who refuses to believe that sexuality is an issue, turning into some kind of sexuality-is-political thinker/activist?

Oh dear. This is new and scary.

I don't care about *issues* and all that sort of stuff. Do I?

I mean, what people do in their personal life is personal, right? It's nothing to do with anyone else. So I've always believed, anyway. And I don't want to have to take a political stance *on the people I fall for*, for God's sake.

"Emily, can I get you anything?" Barry's mother asks.

"No, thanks," I say. "I'm okay."

Except for the thoughts swirling around in my head, of course. I think I'll go back to kissing Barry. It's much simpler.

CHAPTER FIFTY-SEVEN

I am reading the introduction to the *Velvet Goldmine* screenplay in which Todd Haynes talks about sexuality influencing who you are, and I am not sure whether I like this idea or not.

Gay rights and women's rights and all that stuff, and yeah, I *care*, but not enough to do something about it, not enough to think deeply on the matter or go to a protest or take a stand.

I'd make a movie, maybe, to make a point, but should movies have a political agenda behind them? People want to be entertained, not educated. No one watches a movie to feel like they're back in school, being told what to believe in.

I'm glad tomorrow's Friday and I can go out and get drunk and not have to think for a while.

CHAPTER FIFTY-EIGHT

And so on Friday night we are dressed up and ready for action, me and Barry and Roisín and Andrew-and-Lucy. It's a weird group dynamic, with Andrew and Lucy being more couple-ish than ever, if that's even possible, and then me and Barry trying not to be overly affectionate to one another so that Roisín doesn't feel

138

too awkward, and the fact that there are five, not six of us. Hugh's going out with Fiona and her friends. We'll probably see them later. The good (or bad) thing about the size of Dublin is that when you're under eighteen, you tend to run into almost everyone you know when you go out for the night.

I find myself dancing with Barry. He hasn't taken his hands off me ever since we got here, almost as if he's afraid he'll lose me if he lets go for a minute. Either we're holding hands, or he has his arm around me, or *something*. I'm starting to feel claustrophobic. He's never been like this before; does the fact that we're kissing now change *everything*? It's so stupid. We've known each other forever and suddenly all the rules have changed, when the whole reason that we're together now is because we got along so well as friends. The logic of that defies me.

But I do *like* the way his arms feel around me when we dance so closely that we should be oblivious to everything and everyone around us. 'Should be', because I can't manage to block the world out, and something about that doesn't seem right to me. He's giving me his full attention and I'm only half-here, thinking about Roisín and whether she's okay or feeling left out of things, and about Lucy's Debs dress (she hasn't bought one yet; she should probably get a white one so she can re-use it as a wedding dress), and about all kinds of things that I should be forgetting about when I'm trying to have a good time.

I should be happy, right? This is Barry. I'm crazy about Barry. We're going to live together in our stylish apartment someday and be essential parts of each other's lives and never be apart.

And it's so, so easy to mistake intimate friendship for attraction when you're looking for someone to fall for.

CHAPTER FIFTY-NINE

I am in Barry's arms and my head is buried in his shoulder and all I can think is, *Oh, holy crap*.

Rebound girl strikes again. I can't believe what I've done.

Maybe it's a mistake. Maybe I really *am* attracted to Barry and I'm just scared of admitting it to myself, so . . .

No. That's not the way it is. It's me playing mind games with the person I care most about in the whole world. It's just like Declan said, even though it sickens me to admit that he's right.

It's me needing someone to obsess over because that's what I *do*, that's how I function, constantly looking for someone else to develop a crush on in the search for happiness and true love.

And it couldn't be Lucy and it couldn't be Abi and it was so easy for it to be Barry because it's Barry, and I adore him, and respect him, and everyone *expected* it.

It's hard not to do what people expect of you. You start to see yourself and your life through their eyes. Especially when it's your friends, because you love your friends, and their opinions mean so much to you – but it doesn't make it right or real or true.

It doesn't make me in love with Barry.

Because if I were really in love with him, I wouldn't have this sense of being trapped, of having a niggling feeling that something about this is wrong, that I love the intimacy but it can never be sexual between us, because I don't feel that way about him and I'd give anything in the world not to hurt him.

Yeah, it's too late for *that*, isn't it?

Chapter Sixty

And of course once I've realised this, everything's different. To him, nothing has changed, and we're still dancing, still a couple, still Barry-and-Emily or Emily-and-Barry, but for me – it's like I've stepped into an alternative universe.

To everyone else Barry-and-Emily makes sense, and I'm the only one who sees that it doesn't fit, that it's not going to work.

And even *he* doesn't see it, because he has feelings for me, and everybody knows it, and what kind of an ungrateful bitch am I not to appreciate this amazing person who cares so much about me and makes me laugh and makes me feel safe?

But I do appreciate him, I do . . .

. . . I just don't want to sleep with him.

I have to tell him. The longer I put it off, the harder it's going to be. Doing it so early is going to seem ridiculous – but maybe the shorter our 'involvement' is, the easier it will be for people to forget. For him to forget. For everything to go back to normal.

Maybe he'll be secretly relieved. Oh, I hope. Wouldn't that be perfect? I'll say, "Look, Barry, I don't think this is going to work out . . ." and he'll grin and say, "Yeah, I know what you mean. What were we thinking?" and we'll go back to rolling our eyes at the people who think there's a 'spark'.

I mean, what we have amounts to only a few kisses. It doesn't mean anything, right?

And I start working myself up to the speech I'm going to have to give to him at the end of the night.

CHAPTER SIXTY-ONE

"Okay, what is it?" he asks. We are in his house and he looks appropriately apprehensive. Boys understand what "We need to talk" means. It's the universal code for "Prepare to be dumped".

142

"I –" I begin, and falter. I look at him – beautiful, beautiful Barry and realise this is going to hurt.

Last summer. Lying out in the sun with Barry in his back garden, rubbing suntan lotion into his shoulders, and he said, "Jeremy's coming over tonight."

"Cool. You guys going to do anything exciting?" I asked. "Apart from the usual, of course . . ."

"Dirty mind, Em."

"Yeah. It's a gift."

"Actually, we're just going to watch a movie. You should come over too."

"And be the third wheel? No, thanks," I said honestly.

"We'll behave, I promise," he grinned. "No, I just want you to meet him. You're my best friend. I want you to at least know him."

"You just want to show him off, don't you?" I teased.

"Sort of, yeah."

And we laughed, and I was happy that if he was showing Jeremy off, it was to me. That I was important enough for that.

October. I marvelled at his mother's ignorance of her son's life and stayed over his room two nights after the break-up. Barry and I didn't talk much. I crawled into bed with him and we held each other and fell asleep like that. I couldn't do much to cheer him up or make up for the fact that Jeremy was an asshole who cared more about what his friends thought

than about Barry, but I could be there for him, something to
hold onto, always there.

"I think –" I begin, and stop again. God, it's one thing
to make up a speech in your head, and quite another
thing to deliver it to someone. "Barry, you're the best
friend I've ever had – " I try.

And I can see by the look on his face that he already
understands what's coming. I stop, because I can't
make myself say it. I can't because I think I'm going to
cry. That *look* on his face is making my throat tighten.

He doesn't say anything. And I don't say anything.
And we're just looking at one another, and we know
what the story is.

I reach out and try to hug him and he pushes me
away. "Get out," he says coldly.

And I do.

CHAPTER SIXTY-TWO

It's four in the morning and I can't sleep.

I keep checking my phone to see if Barry replies to
any of my text messages. He's ignored all of them. I've
apologised a hundred times and he doesn't care.

I can't say I blame him. What's 'sorry' going to do at
this stage?

Everything's just so messed up. And I mean everything, from Abi to Lucy to Declan to Barry . . . and I don't know what I want.

There's the honest truth. *I don't know what I want.*

I want what I can't have, and when I have it, I don't want it any more. I do whatever the hell I feel like – and then chalk it all up to a learning experience. Never mind the hurt feelings and the lasting consequences, it's all about following your instincts, right?

I hate myself right now. I'm thinking about Barry and even Declan and hating myself for being everything Declan thinks I am, a bitch who messes with people's heads for her own amusement, someone who doesn't care about anyone but herself.

He'd be glad, you know, because now I get it. Finally, Declan, I get it. I get the seething hatred bubbling up inside yourself and how it feels that there is no possible way to deal with it other than doing something big and dramatic like gulping down a bottle of pills or letting a cigarette burn into your flesh. Because it feels so *bad*, and so *awful*, that there's nothing else you *can* do. The tears aren't enough, they keep coming and coming but they're never going to express fully what's inside you.

I'm thinking of Barry and how he must hate me and how *cold* he sounded, like I was no better than dirt beneath his feet, and crying is not enough. I need to *do* something.

And at the same time I don't think I have the energy

to even move from my bed.

Somewhere around half-six, I fall asleep.

CHAPTER SIXTY-THREE

I must be looking particularly depressed on Saturday morning, because even my mother notices something's wrong.

"What are you moping about?" she asks.

"I'm not *moping*," I snap. I'm tempted to say a lot more, but I keep my mouth shut instead.

When you think about it, it's amazing how little people who share your blood can know about you. Parents – they think they know you, they assume that you're just like they were when they were growing up, probably, but they really don't have a clue.

As for Janet – well, she was the perfect child, wasn't she?

I *can't* be perfect. Even if I was a great student and never got into any trouble, I'm still intrinsically flawed. I'm selfish and inconsiderate and oh *yes*, I play mind games with people and screw them up.

I also kiss girls, parents dearest. How do you feel about that? Is it 'just a phase' or is it something that needs to be 'fixed' or is it just 'wrong'? I still like boys, though – does that make it better or worse? Easier to confront or harder?

146

(God, I hate my life.)

I try calling Barry, but his phone just rings and rings. He's never going to speak to me again, is he?

That's nearly five years of friendship down the drain because I make stupid decisions. I am completely disgusted with myself.

CHAPTER SIXTY-FOUR

I end up calling Lucy and she comes over after she's had lunch. We go up to my room, and I can't help but think that I'm glad Janet isn't here to spy on us.

"I broke up with Barry," I say.

"What? Oh, Em, honey, why?"

"It just – I don't know, it just didn't *feel* right." Sitting here, talking to her, I can feel all the thoughts rushing through my head about to spill out. "But maybe that was selfish of me, maybe I should have given it a chance, maybe it could've worked out and he wouldn't hate me right now . . ."

"Give him time. He'll get over it," she says.

"What if he doesn't? What if he stays angry with me, and we just stop talking? It happens, Lucy. You know it does."

"Barry cares about you too much to let that happen, you know that. And you care about him. Don't you?"

I nod. "He's my best friend. Of course, I do."

"These things happen – people screw up, make mistakes. It's no big deal. We all do it." She sounds terribly nonchalant and blasé about the whole thing. I suppose she would, but I don't know how she can be. I mean, these are people's feelings we're talking about.

People's feelings. Right. Because I cared about Declan's feelings so much, didn't I? He doesn't matter, because he's always so melodramatic anyway and it doesn't take much to get him started.

I am such a hypocrite. I hate it when people mess around with me but I'll gladly do it to others. Pot, meet Mr Kettle, I think you two will find you have a lot in common . . .

"You do," I say softly.

Lucy looks at me in surprise. "What?"

"Screw up," I elaborate.

"Thanks, Emily," she frowns. "I really needed to hear that. What on *earth* are you talking about?"

"You cheat on Andrew all the time and he's willing to forgive you because he loves you and because you always say it's a mistake. Well, guess what, Lucy. After a while these things stop being mistakes and it's just you doing whatever the hell you want to do because you're beautiful and charming and you know you can get away with it." And I think I might be just ready to cry again. Oh, for God's *sake*.

"What's going on here?" she exclaims in frustration, before she realises. "Oh, this is about you and me, isn't it?"

"No." Lie. It wasn't meant to be. But it is.

It's about the fact that she kissed me last weekend and then got engaged to her boyfriend. That's what it's about. Or the way she's always used me whenever she sees fit, the way I've learned to use people.

God, I hate epiphanies. They're all about the things that you try to ignore and pretend don't exist coming to the surface and making you realise what a horrible person you really are.

"Emily, I –"

She is hurt and defensive and angry, and I'm on the verge of tears, and she's engaged, and I've just broken my best friend's heart, and clearly the worst thing in the world would be if I kissed her right now.

But I do have a tendency to make stupid decisions.

CHAPTER SIXTY-FIVE

Transition Year, sitting outside with Roisín at lunch-time.

"Hey, was that your boyfriend I saw you with in town?" she asked.

"I don't have a boyfriend," I said, puzzled. "When was this?"

"Last weekend. I waved, but I think you were too wrapped up in him to notice –"

"Oh, that was Barry," I said. "We're just friends."

"Really? You seemed really close for 'just friends'," she smiled.

"Nah, we really are. He's one of those people that you know you're going to be friends with forever but who you'd never actually go out with because you know each other too well, you know?"

"Ah, right," she nodded. There was a pause and then, "So who's the person you keep texting, then, if you don't have a boyfriend?"

The person was Natasha. I'd forgotten Roisín had asked about who I was texting and that I'd answered, in vague terms, that it was just someone I was sort of going out with. I wasn't lying, exactly, just – being selective about the truth.

"Just someone," I said vaguely again.

"And does this person have a name?" she asked, clearly intrigued.

"Her name is Natasha," I said finally, somewhat defiantly, as if I was challenging her to be shocked.

"And where does she go to school?" Roisín asked.

I was thrown by this. "What?"

"Where does she go to school?" she repeated.

"St Anne's," I said. "Um – shouldn't you be freaking out right about now?"

"What, because you have a girlfriend?" she asked. "I sort of suspected it, so . . ."

"Oh."

"Well, considering you kept on saying 'someone' . . . I figured you wouldn't be doing that unless you were trying

150

to hide something."

"I wasn't trying to hide something," I sighed. "I mean, I was, a little, but that's only because — well, you know what the girls in this school are like. Most of them would freak out."

"It's got to be hard for you," she said sympathetically.

It felt almost like pity, and I didn't like that. "Not really," I said firmly. "I don't care. It's just that I don't really see the point in making an unnecessarily big deal out of something that isn't that important, you know? I just want to save myself the hassle."

She nodded. "Seems like a pretty good attitude to have, I guess."

After I got to know her a bit better, we talked about Lucy.

"First girl I ever kissed. First girl I ever knew I liked. Not the first girl I ever slept with, but the first that really mattered. Of course, she had a boyfriend at the time."

Roisín looked a little shocked by this. And this was the edited version of events.

"Things were messed up then," I elaborated, trying to justify it. "She was really upset, and I was just so crazy about her that I would have gone along with anything she asked me to do."

"And did her boyfriend ever find out?"

"Yeah. It was a while afterwards, though, and they'd been

through a lot together since then, so it wasn't a big deal. I mean, they had a fight about it, but it lasted less than a day. They have a really strong relationship. It's great. Really amazing."

"You sound kind of jealous," she noted.

I laughed as if it was a ridiculous suggestion, and avoided giving a real answer.

CHAPTER SIXTY-SIX

"Oh, crap."

"What is it?" I say, stretching out lazily, loving the sensation of bare flesh next to flesh. God, her skin is so soft. I'm tracing circles on her forearm and she – is getting up and pulling on her clothes. "Crap," she repeats.

She has to be somewhere, I surmise, and she's going to be late. That's what it is.

The land of denial is a fun place to be.

"I can't believe –" she starts, and looks at me. "Oh, God, Emily, we shouldn't have –"

"Done that?" I finish for her. I think she's taking her lines from the "Ten Things Not To Say To A Girl Immediately After Sleeping With Her" book.

"You *know* we shouldn't have," she says.

I do. I do know this. Logically I know this. And then there's the non-logical part of me, and all it wants to do is grab her and make her come back to bed and fall asleep in her arms.

"I'll talk to you – soon," she says, slipping her feet into her shoes.

"Are you going to tell Andrew?" I ask, sitting up.

She stares at the floor for a second. "No. I can't. It'll hurt him too much."

"You never worried about that before," I say with just a tinge of bitterness in my voice.

"Things were different then," she says. She's looking at her hands. Her engagement ring.

"See you, Emily," she says, and leaves.

The CD player is still blasting away, blocking out any noise the parents might have heard. Placebo, 'Every You Every Me', and I think the ache is back.

Chapter Sixty-Seven

Declan calls me that night and invites me to a party one of his friends from school is having. I am tempted to make a snide comment about how amazing it is that these friends who he accuses of hating him deep down still manage to invite him out, but before there's a suitable opening, he starts talking: about how he's only been invited because he was there when they were all talking about the party and how he couldn't really have not been invited after that, but that it's clear that he's not really wanted, and that he thought I might like to come along, and we can perhaps have a talk . . .

It's truly amazing how he forgets that we're supposed to be fighting when he wants something out of me. I am tempted to go and get horribly drunk and forget about everything else in my life, but then I contemplate the thought of having this talk that Declan so wants to have with me, which will involve me telling him that sex doesn't matter and him saying that it does, and me being generally hypocritical about the whole thing because it *does* matter when I want it to, so instead I refuse the offer.

He's huffy. He will, eventually, get over it.

And if not, good riddance. I'm sick of looking out for him. I'm not responsible for what he does. I have enough to worry about.

I decide to watch a movie to try to take my mind off things, but it seems like I can't even find shelter in them any more. Either they're movies I've watched with Barry and know that if I watch them now, I'll hear his commentary in my head, or they're movies with pretty heroines that remind me of Lucy, or they're incredibly depressing to begin with. So I end up lying on my bed listlessly, and alternating between running through the events of the last few weeks in my mind, and trying to block it all out completely.

I wonder what love really is. Does Lucy really love Andrew? I mean, she must – but then why isn't she faithful to him? And I know he loves her, but if that means forgiving someone for cheating on you several times – well, if that's love then I'm not sure it's such a wonderful thing.

I wonder if Lucy will end up telling Andrew about what happened anyway.

I wonder what Barry would say if he found out. He'd probably call me a slut. He'd probably be right.

I wonder if it'll all be better in the morning. I hope so.

Chapter Sixty-Eight

The homework is piled up on the desk and all I can think of is that my life is too much right now without having to think about school. I just don't care. I'm going to be in trouble for not doing any of it, but I'll live. The teachers just don't understand. They forget what it's like to be young, to have more pressing concerns than algebra and irregular verbs.

I try calling Barry again, but there is no answer at his house or on his mobile. In a way I'm slightly relieved. When we do talk it's going to be awful.

I want to step out of my life for a couple of weeks and return when everything's been sorted out. I'm annoyed that I can't.

Why does Barry have to take things so seriously? Why doesn't Lucy take *anything* seriously? And why is it so hard to find a happy medium?

At about two o'clock I get a text message telling me there's a message left on my voice mail. The message is from last night. You have to love their punctuality; it closely resembles mine.

Drunken, angry voice. *"Thanks a lot, Emily."*

That's it. The whole message. I'm surprised. Drunken messages are usually a lot more rambling and drawn-out. It sounds like he accidentally hung up before he meant to, but I can't tell what he was about to say next.

So Lucy ended up telling Andrew after all. Well. I think I can honestly say that this is not good.

I turn off my phone and sit on my bed biting my nails. I don't realise, until I'm called downstairs for dinner, that I've been sitting there, barely moving, just thinking and biting, for nearly two hours.

CHAPTER SIXTY-NINE

It started with Hugh.

It's hard to trace things back to their origins. I mean, you can look at your life and say, well, it started when I was born. But it didn't. Really, it started when you were conceived. Or maybe it really started when your parents met for the first time, because if that hadn't happened, you wouldn't be here.

But I think – I think it started with Hugh. I don't

mean being friends with him, or having a crush on him when I was younger – do I? – but going out with him.

Because at the beginning, I was so crazy about him. I really did care about him, and everyone knew it. I thought, I really thought that we were going to live happily ever after.

And then because I was experienced and he wasn't, because I had my sordid past, the things I'd done because I wanted to impress Lucy's friends, and he didn't. He was waiting for the person he loved, he was waiting for the right time, and I just didn't get it. And I didn't see us drifting apart, and I didn't realise that things were eventually going to crumble.

I shouldn't have let him manipulate me the way he did, though.

You want to know why I was crying? Okay, then, I'll tell you. Because I was *angry*, that's why. Because I felt used and sick and dirty and disgusting and a common tramp, and most of all a *victim*.

A helpless scared little girl who lets men do whatever they want to her. And God, I hate myself for it. I hate feeling like that. I hate the fact that I let it happen, that I didn't say, "No, Hugh, you asshole, I'm not going to buy into your 'you're such a tease' bullshit, and that's what it is, bullshit, so go home, okay?" That's what I'd advise someone else to say, that's what the characters in my movies would say, and instead I fell for it and I gave him exactly what he wanted.

And then I didn't want to be a victim any more.

And then there was the rebound girl, and then there was the misguided-attempt-at-comfort guy, and then there was the best friend, and then there was the ex-obsession . . . and now there's me.

Just me, left with one hell of a mess and a considerable number of friendships in tatters.

Not to mention one hell of a headache from figuring all this out.

CHAPTER SEVENTY

I hate Mondays.

I really, really, really hate Mondays.

We have three and a half weeks of classes, our end-of-year Mass and our summer tests left until the holidays.

I work out the hours left in school. Then the minutes.

How the hell is anyone supposed to listen in Maths when their life is in ruins? A little consideration would be nice, you know. The teachers go easy on the students if they know there's someone sick at home, or if their parents have split up or something. But everything else you can handle, apparently, because it's just stupid teenage stuff.

I hate all grown-ups.

I quite possibly also hate all men.

And most of the women on the planet, too. Including myself.

When I check my phone at break-time I have a text message from Declan. He's bitter and hates me. Or something. It's the same old story, and I start to feel angry. I want to scream and shout at him, but seeing as he isn't here, and I have no intention of walking out of school again for his benefit, or yelling down the phone, I text him back. I have quite a lot to say, so it spills out into several messages. That's probably the last of my credit for this week gone, I think.

I am so sick of your shit, Declan. You're self-absorbed, you get attention any way you can without thinking about the effect it has on people who care about you, and you don't appreciate anything in your life. If you're really depressed then go see someone who can really help you. Don't use the people who are trying to be your friends as therapists. Personally I think you're just a spoiled self-pitying brat. I'm sorry you think I was playing with your mind, because I wasn't. You know me, you know what I'm like, and it was downright arrogant of you to think that I was going to make an exception for you. I really am sorry if I hurt you, but what you've put me through all the time I've known you, under the guise of 'friendship', is just as bad, if not worse. It's been nice knowing you.

P.S. Life is an amazing thing – do yourself a favour and appreciate it instead of moping.

And, you know, I think I might even take some of my own advice myself.

CHAPTER SEVENTY-ONE

Roisín and I are walking to the shop at lunch-time when we pass by Lucy with a couple of girls from her class.

Lucy and I avoid each other's eyes, and continue walking.

Roisín smiles at her, looks at me in confusion, and as soon as we're out of earshot asks, "Emily, what's going on?"

I shrug. "It's nothing."

"The same nothing that's had you depressed all day?" she asks.

"Yeah," I say.

"Okay," she says, and she takes a deep breath, like she's about to make a big speech, "I know I'm not as 'cool' as most of your friends, and I haven't done all the things you guys have done, but it doesn't mean that you can't talk to me. I mean, you're probably the closest friend I have, and I – I just wish you'd *tell* me things."

"You'd be shocked and appalled," I say, trying to make a joke out of it. Maybe not a joke. She *does* get shocked.

"I wouldn't," she says.

"Yes! You would! You *do.* You think I'm a slut."

"I don't think you're a slut, Em," she says.

"Oh, really?" I say, not believing her for a minute. "I slept with Declan, did you know that? And guess why I'm not talking to Lucy? Same reason! *Now* what do you think of me?"

She takes a moment to answer. "I'm worried about you."

"You're worried? Why?" I'm confused. This isn't what I was expecting.

"Because I don't think you'd have got involved with either of them unless there was something wrong. I mean, Declan? You hate him. And Lucy's going out with Andrew. They're *engaged,* for God's sake . . . and what about Barry?"

"I broke up with him," I say.

Her eyes widen in surprise. "But –"

"If you mention that 'spark' thing again, I will hit you," I say firmly.

She wisely decides not to mention it. "*Is* there something wrong?"

"No. Not really. Just my bad decision-making skills. And then – I don't know, there was the whole thing with Hugh, and that's sort of had me messed up for the last while and doing stupid things." She thinks I mean the break-up. I'm not going to correct her. It's that too. It's the entire situation.

Roisín is quiet for a while. I look at her impatiently. "Come on, say something," I say.

"I can't believe you slept with *Declan*," she says eventually, wrinkling her nose in revulsion.

I burst out laughing, and then hug her tightly.

CHAPTER SEVENTY-TWO

Andrew and Lucy have broken up and called off their engagement. I learn of this on Tuesday evening, when I'm over at Shane's house. His band are having a practice, and they wanted a few honest critics there. Fiona, Abi and I are sitting around listening to them, but they only play one song before we end up all gossiping.

"What did you think?" I murmur to Abi while Fiona is praising Hugh excessively.

"They have potential," she says diplomatically, smiling.

I grin. I must admit I entertained vague hopes of them being brilliant, so that they could do the soundtrack for my first movie or something, but it's not looking like such a possibility any more.

"Hey, Emily, did you hear about Lucy and Andrew?" Shane asks me.

I shake my head. "I haven't been talking to them in the last few days."

"They broke up," he says.

It takes me a moment to absorb this. When I do, my internal response is short and simple: *Oh, crap.*

Fiona frowns. "Weren't they, like, engaged?"

Hugh seems surprised by this too. "Yeah, they were. What happened?"

"Lucy cheated on him," Shane says, clearly enjoying being the centre of attention now.

"With you?" Hugh and Caroline ask at the same time. Sarah doesn't look too thrilled at the fact that they suspect her boyfriend right away.

"No, not with me," he says, exasperated. "But that's what Andrew thought. He picked a fight with me."

"Hold on. When did this happen?" Fiona asks. We're all listening to him attentively now, even though I'm not sure I really like discussing this topic. Shane must know it's me. I'm going to kill him for bringing this up.

"Saturday night," Sarah fills in. "We were all at Philip's house, and Lucy and Andrew were upstairs in one of the bedrooms –"

"– and naturally, we all thought they were just enjoying themselves," Shane grins. "But then they came downstairs, and Lucy was crying, and Andrew just walks over to me and says, 'I want to talk to you' and looking like he's ready for a fight, and I say I don't know what he's talking about, and he moves like he's going to hit me, but I block it, and then I –"

Shane goes on about his heroic role in the fight for a while before getting back on topic. Why is it that guys always boast about these things? Don't they realise that any sensible person just tunes out?

"– but then Lucy says that it wasn't me, and she yells at him for picking on me, and then he starts shouting at her for the time she met me, and then she says that they're leaving, and that she'll tell him who it was on the way home."

I let out a quiet sigh of relief. He doesn't know.

"And then he said that couldn't ever get married to someone who treats him like that," Sarah continues, "and she said she couldn't ever get married to someone as irrational as he was, blah blah blah, and we could still hear them screaming at each other as they were walking down the road."

"I wonder who it was," Hugh says.

"Might have been someone from school," Sarah muses.

The blonde girl, Caroline, looks up in surprise. "Is Lucy bi?"

"No, Lucy's an opportunist," Shane grins.

Hugh and Abi look at me to see how I'll react to this. I shrug. "It's true. She is."

"Have you any idea who it might've been, Em?" Hugh asks.

"No, would you stop pestering me? It's none of your business," I snap.

Silence.

Nothing says 'I probably do know and I just don't

want to talk about it, quite possibly because it was me and I'm terribly sensitive about this and to make matters worse I have issues with you, Hugh, so I'm going to lash out at you over something trivial' like what I've just said, I think. And they all know it.

I try a weak smile. "Sorry. Just – it's Lucy's private life, you know?"

Hugh nods. "Yeah. Sorry, I didn't mean to –"

"It's okay," I say quickly.

Oh, the awkwardness. So much for being over the break-up with Hugh.

Sarah intervenes. "So, great weather we've been having," she grins.

We all start laughing.

"Hey, you guys should play the song Hugh wrote," Fiona suggests.

I hope it doesn't involve him trying to sing. Of course, Fiona seems to think he's wonderful at everything. She's such a devoted girlfriend. Or a groupie. Whichever way you want to look at it.

"Maybe later," Shane says vaguely. I can't help but smirk.

Everyone starts leaving around ten. I'm getting my coat when Shane says, "Hey, can you hold on a sec?"

"Sure," I say, waving goodbye to the others. "What is it?"

"Everything okay with you and Hugh?" he asks.

I shrug. "Yeah, it's okay, I just overreacted earlier."

"He said the two of you haven't talked properly ever since you broke up."

"Nope, we haven't," I say.

"You should," he says.

"Don't even try lecturing me, Shane," I grin.

He laughs. "Okay, I won't. Hey – it was you, wasn't it?"

"With Lucy?" Well, since everyone already suspects it, I nod. "Yeah."

"I probably would have done the same thing," he says.

I roll my eyes. "Yeah, *you* would have, I'm sure."

He shrugs. "She's hot."

"Does your girlfriend know that you think Lucy's hot?" I say pointedly.

"Don't even try lecturing me, Emily," Shane smirks.

I hug him. "I'll see ya."

"Yeah, see ya," he smiles.

CHAPTER SEVENTY-THREE

I see Lucy at lunch-time on Wednesday and call out, "Hey" and wave her over.

"I heard you and Andrew broke up," I say. "I'm sorry."

She bites her lip. "Well, it was never going to last

forever anyway, was it? It was stupid of us to think that it would."

"If you need to talk –" I say.

"Yeah, thanks," she smiles, but I have a feeling she just wants to get away from me. In a way I'm relieved when she goes back to her friends. I've done my duty. I think spending time with her right now would probably make the situation worse, anyway.

Now that the initial stage of self-loathing has passed, I find myself feeling guilty about not feeling as guilty as I think I should about my contribution to their break-up. It's silly, I suppose. It's okay to think that it's mostly her fault, isn't it? I mean, she's the one in the relationship, and I didn't force her to do anything. Her decision, not mine.

Some part of me is even happy that they're not engaged any more, because I don't think they were ready for it. And I have a feeling that their break-up isn't going to be permanent, because they care too much about one another to let it be.

I go over to Barry's house in the evening with *Bring It On* under my arm. "Peace offering," I say when he opens the door. "Cheerleading fun?"

He sighs. "Emily, I really don't want to talk to you right now."

"Do you hate me?" I ask quietly.

"No," he says after a moment, "but I need some time."

"Okay," I nod, and I try to hug him. He lets me, and I hold onto him for a while before letting go.

CHAPTER SEVENTY-FOUR

Lose yourself in the beat. Lose yourself in the music and you can forget that your boyfriend's checking out another girl, I thought to myself.

What did I care, anyway, if he liked Fiona? I didn't want him to be with me if he didn't want it, out of some sense of duty. I could have a good time even without him. There were a couple of girls from school there and there was a group of us dancing together, just enjoying the music. I pulled Hugh closer and whispered in his ear, "Look, just do whatever you want, okay?"

He looked confused. "What are you talking about?"

"You've been staring at Fiona all night. If you like her, just go for it. I don't care anymore."

He stared at me for a moment. "Are you mad at me or something?"

"No," I said patiently, and then continued to dance, watching Abi and her boyfriend out of the corner of my eye.

Somehow, even though I'm not really talking to Barry, I feel better just knowing that he doesn't hate me. Everything's going to be okay. It's not the end of the world. My friendship with him isn't ruined forever.

It makes me feel like I can face – well, maybe not *anything*, but some things.

And so I'm waiting at Hugh's door. His dad answers and lets me in, calling Hugh from upstairs.

I feel weird being in this house, like I don't really belong now that Hugh and I aren't going out, even though it was almost like a second home to me when I was younger.

"Heya," he says, looking startled to see me.

"Hey," I say.

He hovers for a moment, not sure whether to sit beside me on the couch or take the armchair. In the end he opts for the armchair. "So . . ." he prompts.

I give him a small smile. "I just wanted to apologise for last night," I start. "I was –"

"Nah, I shouldn't have asked. Don't worry about it," he says.

We sit there awkwardly for a little while before I ask, "So, how are things with Fiona?"

"Great, great," he says. He senses this is his cue. Good boy. "I'm sorry, Em. About Fiona, I mean. I know you said it was okay, but I still feel shitty for going off with her."

"It's okay," I say, because that's what I'm supposed to say. It's amazing how finally hearing those words can make a difference, though.

"And we haven't really talked, and – I miss you," he says.

"I miss you too," I smile, and I get up and hug him.

"I'm sorry for the other thing, too," he says, and I inhale sharply. I didn't know he even realised that that had been an issue.

"It's okay," I say again, because that's as much of an apology as I'm going to get out of him, but it's enough. Enough for me to let go. Forgive but not forget.

CHAPTER SEVENTY-FIVE

It's sunny on Friday and we're sitting outside at lunch-time again. Roisín, Sarah and Fiona are talking about some reality TV show. Abi turns to me and says, "Hey, have you been talking to Declan?"

"I texted him on Monday," I say. "Not since then, no."

"He's starting therapy, you know," she says.

My jaw drops. "What? Seriously?"

She nods. "Yeah, his dad saw his arms and freaked out about it. At first he thought someone else was doing it, but then Declan told him he was doing it to himself, and actually put a cigarette out in his arm in front of his dad, just to prove it –"

"God, he's really messed up," I mutter.

"He has problems, Emily," she says quietly before continuing. "Anyway, he's starting next week, I think."

"Good for him," I say. "Though I suppose he'll be

going around now acting like we should all be really nice to him because he's in *therapy*."

"Oh, stop," she says, but it's only half-hearted, I think. "He's not that bad."

"Did he tell you all this personally?" I ask.

She shrugs. "He texts me sometimes, that's all."

"I see," I say. "When he needs someone to listen to him whine."

"Nah, not really," she says. "He thinks I'm more screwed-up than he is, so he doesn't feel like he can, you know?"

"Still . . . watch out. He can be really draining," I warn her.

"He is messed up," she says, "but I still feel – I don't know . . . like I'm on his side. Do you know what I mean?"

"Yeah, kinda," I say. "How are you doing?" She knows what I mean.

"Doing okay," she smiles.

"Good to hear," I say, and I hug her.

And from somewhere close by I can hear Wendy saying, "God, wouldn't you think they'd give it a break in school?

"Who?" one of her friends asks.

"Emily Keating and her *girlfriend*," she says distastefully.

Abi, Roisín, Sarah and Fiona look at me.

"Can we kill her?" Abi mutters.

"Ignore her," Roisín says at the same time.

I'm already standing up and walking right over there.

"Wendy?" I say sweetly.

She and her friends are smirking. "Yeah?"

"Firstly, Abi's not my girlfriend. Secondly, I was just hugging her. Thirdly – I'm sorry you have a problem with me and my orientation. I have a problem with your very *existence*, so I think we're even. But if you ever talk about me in that tone ever again, I swear I will beat the crap out of you."

She and her friends are still smirking. "Dyke," she says, as I start to walk back to my friends.

Violence is not the answer. Violence is *never* the answer.

So I only hit her once before going back, very calmly, to the others. She's not even hurt and she's too taken aback by it to retaliate until it's too late.

"I think you got your point across," Sarah grins.

"Yeah, I think so," I say, and then we're all laughing.

"Hey, Emily?" Maria calls over. "Way to go."

"Good aim," Christine adds with a smile.

"I can't believe I just did that," I say, as it starts to sink in properly.

"Sorry you did?" Roisín asks.

I shrug. "Nope. She had it coming."

Sarah nods. "She really did. She's a cow."

We eat the rest of our lunch in peace, after the buzz dies down. I can't help but feel a little bit proud for standing up for myself. And my kind. Oh, God, political awareness and gay-rights campaigning, here I come.

Chapter Seventy-Six

Four things of note happen over the weekend.

The first is that I actually do some of the homework that I've been given. I get an Irish essay and French revision questions done.

The second is Janet coming home and telling me that she realises she reacted 'over-harshly' to seeing me and Lucy together, and that she should have been more supportive. I tell her that I'm not going out with Lucy. She seems relieved.

The third is that I actually fill out the application for the film course this summer. I figure it can't hurt, and it feels like another good move, taking a step towards being what I'd like to be.

The fourth is that when I turn on my phone on Sunday morning, there's a missed call from a number I only vaguely recognise. I don't have the number stored on my phone, but I'm pretty sure it's Jeremy's. It's weird that he'd call me. I haven't heard from him in ages, not since he and Barry broke up. I like him, even

if his inability to deal with being gay bothers me sometimes and meant that he was a total asshole towards
Barry.

There's no message, and when I call the number,
there's no answer. I'll call him later. In the meantime,
I'm supposed to be going over to Hugh's house today.

When I get there, there's a few guys in his year there,
with white faces, talking about this guy they knew that
killed himself yesterday. I hear phrases: ". . . can't
believe he . . .", ". . . never saw it coming . . .", "he was
a bit depressed, but I never thought . . ."

My heart starts pounding. Oh, God, Declan. "Who
was it?" I ask them, panicking wildly. Oh God. He's
done it, he's finally done it, and I wasn't able to stop
him. I wasn't there for him. I tried and I tried and in the
end it just wasn't enough, and I can't help but feel as
though it's all my fault.

CHAPTER SEVENTY-SEVEN

"Jeremy Carter," one of them says. "He's – uh, was – in
our year."

Oh. Holy. Crap. No way. My heart starts beating nor-
mally for a second, and then returns to the pounding as
soon as I remember. The phone call.

"Are you going to be okay?" I ask Hugh, who's look-

174

ing pretty shaken. He looks exactly like I feel.

"Yeah," he says.

"I think – I'd be better off going. I don't want to intrude, I mean, I didn't know the guy that well," I say awkwardly.

Except that we used to talk and he called me last night and my phone was switched off and maybe if I'd actually answered that call he'd still be alive. Oh, God.

He nods. "Okay," he says, and I hold him tightly before I leave.

They don't even know that he and Barry knew each other. They avoided each other in school even when they were going out, so no one would suspect anything. Part of me understands why, after the Abi scandal. I have to go and talk to him. I'm in shock; I can't even imagine how badly he must feel.

Shane is leaving Barry's house when I arrive. "Hey, Emily," he says.

"Hey," I say.

"Did you hear?" he asks.

I nod. "Yeah. Does Barry know?"

"Yeah, I came over to tell him. I figured he wouldn't want to hear it over the phone."

I stare at him for a moment. "You know about – the two of them?"

He nods. "Yeah. I think I'm the only one Barry told. Apart from you, I mean."

"Hugh doesn't even – he still thinks Barry's

straight," I say.

"Seriously?" Shane says in surprise. "God."

"Is Barry okay?" I ask.

"I think he's in shock," Shane says. "I would have stayed, but he said he wanted to be alone, so –"

"Oh, maybe I shouldn't –"

"Nah, I think he'll want to see you."

Chapter Seventy-Eight

We are lying on his bed, fully clothed, with the duvet pulled over our heads, and I am holding him as tightly as is humanly possible.

My shoulder is still damp from his tears. The crying's over for the moment. Now all I can do is be here for him.

Every so often he will say something about Jeremy, and I will listen, and stroke his hair, and kiss his forehead. I don't say anything. I don't think there's anything I can say to make him feel better, and the helplessness makes me frustrated.

I stay the night, because the night's the worst time to be alone, and when I leave in the morning he says, "Thanks, Emily."

I don't feel like I should be thanked. He doesn't know about the phone call. I need to tell him, but not now. Not yet.

"Call me if you need to talk," I say quietly, and hug him again before I begin the walk home.

As I walk, I try to tell myself that it is ridiculous to assume that Jeremy's suicide and the fact that he broke up with Barry because he couldn't handle being in a gay relationship are not connected.

I tell myself that everyone has problems. Declan's completely messed up, and he's straight, apart from a bit of under-the-influence experimentation.

And I tell myself that it is okay that I wasn't able to answer his call, that I shouldn't blame myself for his death.

I can't convince myself.

CHAPTER SEVENTY-NINE

I tell him the day before the funeral.

"He called my phone on Saturday night," I say.

Barry knows right away who I'm talking about.

"It was turned off. He didn't leave a message. I –" And I'm crying, at the thought of it – at the thought of it being that simple. No one answers the phone, so go and kill yourself. I know, logically, that it's not my fault, but logic and me have never been particularly great friends and it's very hard to apply logic to a situation where a seventeen-year-old is being buried tomorrow.

This time it's Barry who's comforting me. It makes a change. There's so few people I'll let comfort me; I'm used to being the one who tries to make everything better for everyone else.

"It wasn't your fault," he says.

"But –"

"It's not up to you to sort out everyone else's life," he tells me. "Help out your friends when you can, but don't let it take over your own life, for God's sake."

"I should have been able to stop him."

"It was his choice, Em." He sounds like he's learned this line off by heart, like he's been repeating it to himself over and over. I'm not the only one feeling guilty here. "Look," he continues, "you can't go around trying to save everyone. It doesn't work. Some people don't want to be saved. And sometimes you make things worse."

"Declan," I sigh.

"Declan," he agrees.

I know what he's saying is right. It's a lesson I've tried to learn over and over, but it doesn't stop me from needing to do *something* if I think it might help.

"I'm sorry," I say, "for – everything."

"I know," he says.

And with that, things are okay again. We're okay, and that means a lot to me.

It doesn't make up for not being able to save Jeremy, even though I know everyone's responsible for their own decisions. It doesn't make up for all the complications with Lucy or Declan. It doesn't make up for a lot of things, but it helps. It really does.

I can't go back in time and change things, and there's no point wishing otherwise. I've always tried not to have regrets, and I don't want to start now.

What I *can* do now, I guess, is be there for my friends.

And I can appreciate life, the way I told Declan to, only I'm not sure I really understood what that meant until now. I can figure out what I want to do with mine, while I'm waiting for the person of my dreams to come along – if he or she ever does. I can try to be the sort of person I want to be, and hope for the best.

And who knows, maybe someday we'll all get our fairytale ending.

EPILOGUE

Two weeks after Jeremy's death, Barry will tell his mother the truth about their relationship. She will look at him oddly and wonder why he asked her to sit down. "I knew that," she will say patiently. He will stare at her in shock and will later use this story as an amusing anecdote at parties.

I will also use it as the basis for the short film I make at the course, which will prove to be less like school than I imagined. The teacher will be rather impressed with my work and tell me that I have "real potential", which will be the first time anyone has ever used the word "potential" when speaking to me without it following the words "You're not living up to your full . . ."

Lucy and Andrew will get back together at a party after their exams finish, surprising no one. They will be inseparable all summer and discover in August that they've gotten into the courses they wanted.

Declan will spend his summer writing his feelings down, as his therapist has suggested, in the form of poetry. He will read these poems to Abi, who will smile encouragingly but confess to me that they're terrible.

Hugh and I will become real friends again, and spend so much time together that Fiona will end up picking a fight with me at a party. The two of us will yell at each other for a while, getting so worked up that our friends will worry that we're going to start throwing punches. Roisín will drag me away from her and will kiss me in order to distract me. I will prove to be easily distracted, and will also find myself re-evaluating every thought I've had about her innocence later that night. Barry will claim he saw it coming.

She'll play a modern-day Rapunzel when I finally get around to making my first movie, but she won't be one bit interested in the handsome prince.

And then we will all live, more or less, happily ever after.

THE END

Direct to your home!

If you enjoyed this book why not visit our website:

www.poolbeg.com

and get another book delivered straight to your home or to a friend's home!

www.poolbeg.com

All orders are despatched within 24 hours.

Published by poolbeg.com

Girls on the Verge

THE CLAIRE HENNESSY COLLECTION

Girls on the Verge is a fantastic collection of Claire Hennessy's first three books; Dear Diary, Being her Sister and Memories.

Dear Diary

5 friends, 5 diaries, 5 months. They've got it all down, but do they really know each other? Boyfriends, slumber-parties and stepsisters. In 5 months, 5 diaries and 5 friends come a long way!

Memories

Sometimes it's hard to get over your past . . . Rachel is convinced she's a loser and second best to her sister Danielle. Only one thing will make her happy: to be thin. Danielle is hopelessly devoted to her ex-boyfriend. But he's moved on, with her best friend Nicola . . . which isn't helping their friendship. Nicola is haunted by a humiliating rejection, everyone thinks she is oozing confidence, she thinks she's worthless. One day they'll look back on it as a learning curve, if they survive it all, that is.

Being her Sister

What do you do when life is all about being her sister? When no matter what you do, you end up being compared to her? What do you do if you end up hating her?

ISBN 1-84223-259-2

Published by poolbeg.com

Afterwards

CLAIRE HENNESSY

When 14-year-old Claudia gets home one day to find her mother's walked out, she doesn't know what to think. "I can't do this anymore" is hardly an explanation, and her dad is too busy with work to offer any insight into why his wife has left, nor does he seem to even take it seriously.

Her older brother Ben is no use either – he's too busy hating school and being cool to bother even talking to her, unless he wants something – and her younger sister Julie is engrossed in her sulking and getting into fights.

Her friends have no idea about what's going on – Beth might care, but with Christy never shutting up about her latest boyfriend it's hard to get a word in edgeways, and anyway, maybe some things are better left within the family. Her mum leaving changes everything, and even if she does come back, nothing's ever going to be the same ever again.

ISBN 1-84223-207-X

Published by poolbeg.com

STEREOTYPE

CLAIRE HENNESSY

"Always remember that you are unique. Just like everyone else."

Abigail Evans, transition-year student - a typical neurotic teenager or does she have a real problem?

When she feels empty and to combat the *blahness*, she buys stuff she doesn't really need or want. Well, if she doesn't do that she has to cut herself with razor-blades that leave ugly red scars along the inside of her arm. Then she has to wear long sleeves until the scabs fall off.

But why does she cut herself? She's not from a dysfunctional family, hasn't had a horrible childhood experience and she has friends: Leanne - sarcastic bitchy, Tina - always on a diet, Karen - fits in everywhere.

They all drive her mad.

They are stereotypical teenagers. How boring!

So is it all just melodramatic teen angst or is Abi seriously screwed up and no one is listening?

ISBN 1-84223-165-0